Manslaughter

Alice Duer Miller

ISBN: 978-1-64799-776-2

CONTENTS

CONTENTS

CHAPTER I

Whenever she and Lydia had a scene Miss Bennett thought of the first scene she had witnessed in the Thorne household. She saw before her a vermillion carpet on a mottled marble stair between high, polished-marble walls. There was gilt in the railing, and tall lanky palms stood about in majolica pots. Up this stairway an angry man was carrying an angrier child. Miss Bennett could see that broad back in its heavy blue overcoat, and his neck, above which the hair was still black, crimsoning with fury and exertion. On one side of him she could see the thin arms and clutching hands of the little girl, and on the other the slender kicking legs, expressing passionate rebellion in every spasmodic motion. The clutching hands caught the tip of a palm in passing, and the china pot went rolling down the stairs and crashed to bits, startling the two immense great Dane puppies which had been the occasion of the whole trouble.

The two figures, swaying and struggling, went on up; for though the man was strong, a writhing child of ten is no light burden; and the stairs, for all their grandeur, were steep, and the carpet so thick that the foot sank into it as into new-fallen snow. Just as they passed out of sight Miss Bennett saw the hands of the child, now clenched fists, begin to beat on the man's arms, and she heard the clear, defiant young voice repeating, "I will keep them! I will!" The man's "You won't" was not spoken, but was none the less understood. Miss Bennett knew that when the heads of the stairs was reached the blows would be returned with interest.

Usually in the long struggle between these two indomitable wills Miss Bennett had been on Joe Thorne's side, coarse, violent man though he was, for she was old-fashioned and believed that children ought to obey. But this night he had alienated her sympathy by being rude to her—for the first and last time. He had come home after one of his long absences to the hideous house in Fifth Avenue in which he took so much pride, and had found these two new pets of Lydia's careening about the hall like young calves. He had turned on Miss Bennett.

"What the hell do you let her do such things for?" he had demanded, and Miss Bennett had answered with unusual spirit.

"Because she's so badly brought up, Mr. Thorne, that no one can do anything with her."

Lydia had stood by defiantly, glancing from one to the other, with a hand in the collar of each of her dogs, her face pale, her jaw set, her head not much above the sleek battleship-gray heads of the

1

great Danes, her small body pulled first one way and then the other by their gambols. All the time she was saying over and over, "I will keep them! I will! I will!"

She hadn't kept them; she had lost that particular skirmish in the long war. Not till some years later did she begin to win; but whether she lost or won, Miss Bennett was always conscious of a rush of pity for the slim, black-eyed little girl thrusting her iron will so fearlessly against that of the man from whom she had inherited it.

And for the Lydia of to-day, now engaged in thrusting her will against the will of the world, Miss Bennett felt the same unreasoning pity—pity which rendered her weak in her own defense when any dispute arose between them. She and Lydia had been having a scene now; only a little scene—hardly more than a discussion.

Morson saw it clearly when he came in after luncheon to get the coffee cups, although a complete and decorous silence greeted his entrance. He saw it in the way in which his young employer was standing, as erect as an Indian, looking slantingly down her cheek at her companion. Miss Bennett was sitting on the sofa with her feet in their high-heeled satin slippers crossed, and she was slipping the rings nervously up and down her fine, thin fingers.

She was a small, well-made woman, to whom prettiness had come with her gray hair. The perfection of all her appointments, which might once have been interpreted as the vanity of youth, turned out to be a settled nicety that stood her in good stead in middle life and differentiated her at fifty-five—a neat, elegant little figure among her contemporaries.

The knowledge that he was interrupting a discussion did not hurry Morson any more than the faintest curiosity delayed him. He brushed up the hearth, turned a displaced chair, collected the cups on his tray and left the room at exactly the same pace at which he had entered it. He had known many scenes in his day.

As soon as the door closed behind him Miss Bennett said: "Of course, if you meant you don't want me to ask my friends to your house you are perfectly within your rights, but I could not stay with you, Lydia."

"You know I don't mean that, Benny," said the girl without either anger or apology in her voice. "I'm delighted to have you have anyone at all when I'm not here and anyone amusing when I am. The point is that those old women were tiresome. They bored you and you knew that they were going to bore me. You sacrificed me to make a Roman holiday for them."

Miss Bennett could not let this pass.

2

"You should feel it an honor—a woman like Mrs. Galton, whose work among the female prisoners of this—"

"Noble women, noble women, I have no doubt, but bores, and it makes me feel sick, literally sick, to be bored."

"Don't be coarse, Lydia."

"Sick—here," said Lydia with a sharp dig of her long fingers on her diaphragm. "Let's be clear about this, Benny. I can't stand having my own tiresome friends about, and I will not put up with having yours."

Lydia had come home after a morning of shopping in town. Disagreeable things had happened, only Benny did not know that. She had bought a hat—a tomato-colored hat—had worn it a block and decided it was a mistake, and had gone back and wanted to change it, and the woman had refused to take it back. There had been little consolation in removing her custom from the shop forever—she had been forced to keep the hat. Then motoring back to Long Island a tire had gone, and she had come in late for luncheon to find Benny amiably entertaining the two old ladies.

The very fact that they were, as she said, noble women, that their minds moved with the ponderous exactitude characteristic of so many good executives, made their society all the more trying to Lydia. She wearied of them, wearied, as Mariana in the Moated Grange. She had so often asked Benny not to do this to her and after all it was her house.

"You're very hard, my dear," said her companion—"very hard and very ignorant and very young. If you could only find an interest in such work as Mrs. Galton is doing—"

"Good heavens, was this a benevolent plot on your part to find me an interest?"

Miss Bennett looked dignified and a little stubborn, as if she were accustomed to being misunderstood, as if Lydia ought to have known that she had had a reason for what she did. As a matter of fact, she had no plan; she was not a plotter. That was one of the difficulties between her and Lydia. Lydia arranged her life, controlled her time and her surroundings. Miss Bennett amiably drifted, letting events and her friends control. She could never understand why Lydia held her responsible for situations which it seemed to her simply happened, and yet she could never resist pretending that she had deliberately brought them about. She began to think now that it had been her idea, not Mrs. Galton's, to get Lydia interested in prison reform.

"No one can be happy, Lydia, without an unselfish interest, something outside of themselves."Lydia smiled. There was

3

something pathetic in poor little ineffective Benny trying to arrange her life for her.

"I contrive to be fairly happy, thank you, Benny. I've got to leave you, because I have an engagement at Eleanor's at four, and it's ten minutes before now."

"Lydia, it's ten miles!"

"Ten miles—ten minutes."

"You'll be killed if you drive so recklessly."

"No Benny, because I drive very well."

"You'll be arrested then."

"Even less."

"How can you be so sure?"

That was something that it was better not to tell, so Lydia went away laughing, leaving Miss Bennett to wonder, as she always did after one of these interviews, how it was possible to feel so superior to Lydia when they were apart and so ineffectual when they were together. She always came to the same conclusion—that she was betrayed by her own fineness; that she was more aware of shades, of traditions than this little daughter of a workingman. Lydia was not little. She was half a foot taller than Adeline Bennett's own modest five-feet-two, but the adjective expressed a latent wish. Miss Bennett often introduced it into her descriptions. A nice little man, a clever little woman, a dear little person were some of her favorite tags. They made her bulk larger in her own vision.

The little daughter of the workingman ran upstairs for her hat. She found her maid, Evans, engaged in polishing her jewels. The rite of polishing Miss Thorne's jewels took place in the bathroom, which was also a dressing room, containing long mirrors, a dressing table, cupboards with glass doors through which Miss Thorne's bright hats and beribboned underclothes showed faintly. It was carpeted and curtained and larger than many a hall bedroom.

Here Evans, a pale, wistful English girl, was spreading out the jewelry as she finished each piece, laying them on a white towel where the rays of the afternoon sun fell upon them—the cabochon ruby like a dome of frozen blood, the flat, clear diamond as blue as ice, and the band of emeralds and diamonds for her hair flashing rays of green and orange lights. Lydia liked her jewelry for the best of all reasons—she had bought most of it herself. She particularly liked the emerald band, which made her look like an Eastern princess in a Russian ballet, and in her opinion exactly fitted her type. But her beauty was not so easily classified as she thought. To describe her in words was to describe a picture by Cabanel of The Star of the Harem—such a picture as the galleries of the second half of the nineteenth century were sure to contain—the oval face, the

4

splendid dark eyes, the fine black eyebrows, the raven hair; but Lydia's skin was not transparently white, and a slight heightening of her cheek bones and a thrust forward of her jaw suggested something more Indian than Eastern, something that made her seem more at home on a mountain trail than on the edge of a marble pool.

As she entered, Evans was brushing the last traces of powder from a little diamond bracelet less modern than the other pieces. Lydia took it in her hand.

"I almost forgot I had that," she said.

Three or four years before, when she had first known Bobby Dorset, when they had been very young, he had given it to her. It had been his mother's, and she had worn it constantly for a year or so. An impulse of tenderness made her slip it on her arm now, and as it clung there like a living pressure the heavy feeling of it faintly revived a whole cycle of old emotions. She thought to herself that she had some human affections after all.

"It ought to be reset, miss," said Evans. "The gold spoils the diamonds."

"You do keep my things beautifully, Evans."

The girl colored at the praise, not often given by her rapidly moving young mistress, and the muscles twitched in her throat.

"A hat—any hat, Evans."

She pulled it on with one quick, level glance in the glass, and was gone with the bracelet, half forgotten, on her arm.

During the few minutes that Lydia had been upstairs a conflict had gone on in the mind of Miss Bennett downstairs. Should she be offended or should she be superior? Was it more dignified to be angry because she really could not allow herself to be treated like that? Or should she forgive because she was obviously so much older and wiser than Lydia?

She decided—as she always did—in favor of forgiveness, and as she heard Lydia's quick light footsteps crossing the hall she called out, "Don't drive the little car too fast!"

"Not over sixty," Lydia's voice answered.

As she sprang into the gray runabout waiting at the door with its front wheels turned invitingly outward, pressed on the self-starter with her foot, slid the gears in without a sound, it looked as if she intended her reply to be taken literally. But the speedometer registered only thirty on her own drive—thirty-five as she straightened out on the highway. As she said, she never drove fast without a good reason.

Like most people of her type and situation, Lydia was habitually late. The reason she gave to herself was that she crowded

5

a little more activity into the twenty-four hours than those who managed to be on time. But the true reason was that she preferred to be waited for rather than to run any risk of waiting herself. It seemed a distinct humiliation to her that she should await anyone else's convenience. To-day, however, she had a motive for being on time—that is to say, not more than twenty minutes late. They were going to play bridge at Eleanor's and Bobby would be there; and for some reason she never understood it fussed Bobby if she were late and everyone began abusing her behind her back; and if Bobby were fussed he lost money, and he couldn't afford to lose it. She hated Bobby to lose money—minded it for him more than he minded it for himself.

One of the facts that she saw most clearly in regard to her own life was that the man she married must be a man of importance, not only because her friends expected that of her but because she needed a purpose, a heightened interest—a great man in her life. Yet strangely enough the only men to whom her heart had ever softened were idle, worthless men, of whom Bobby was only a sample. Among women she liked the positive qualities—courage, brilliance, achievement; but among men she seemed to have selected those who needed a strong controlling hand upon their destiny. Benny said it was the maternal in her, but less friendly critics said it was the boss. Perhaps the two are not so dissociated as is generally thought. Lydia repudiated the maternal explanation without finding another. Only she knew that the very thing that made her fond of men like Bobby prevented her falling in love with them; whereas the men with whom it seemed possible to fall in love were men with whom she always quarreled, so that instead of love there was not even friendship.

Some years before she had been actually engaged to be married—though the engagement had never been announced—to an Englishman, a thin, hawk-faced man, the Marquis of Ilseboro. She was not in love with him, though he was a man with whom women did fall in love. Benny had been crazy about him. He was companionable in a silent sort of way, made love to her with extreme assurance and knew a great deal about life and women.

But from the very first their two wills had clashed in small matters—in questions of invitations, manners, Lydia's dress. Again and again Ilseboro had yielded, but yielded with a deliberation that gave no suggestion of defeat. These struggles which go on out of sight and below consciousness in most relations are never decided by the actual event but by the strength of position in which the combatants are left. Benny, for instance, sometimes did the most rebellious things, but did them in a sort of frenzy of panic, followed by unsought explanations. Ilseboro was just the reverse. He yielded because he had a positive wish to adjust himself, as far as possible, to her wishes. Lydia began to be not afraid of him, for like Caesar she was not liable to fear, but dimly aware that his was a stronger nature than her own. This means either love or hate. There had been a few hours one evening when she had felt grateful, admiring, eager to give up; when if she had loved him at all she could have worshiped him. But she did not love him, and when she saw that what he was looking forward to was fitting her into a niche which he'd been building for centuries for the wives of the Ilseboros she really hated him.

Ever since her childhood the prospect of laying aside her own will had stirred her to revolt. She could still remember waking herself up with a start in terror at the thought that in sleep she would doff her will for so many hours. Later her father had wished to send her to a fashionable boarding school; but she had made such wild scenes at the idea of being shut up—of being one of a community—that the plan had been given up. She would have married anyone in order to be free, but being already uncommonly free she rebelled at the idea of giving up her individuality by marriage, particularly by marriage with Ilseboro. She broke her engagement. Ilseboro had loved her and made himself disagreeable. She never forgot the parting curse he put upon her.

"The trouble with being such a damned bully as you are, my dear Lydia," he said, "is that you'll always get such second-rate playmates."

She answered that no one ought to know better than he did. His manner to her servants had long secretly shocked her. He spoke to them without one shade of humanity in his tone, yet oddly enough they all liked him except the chauffeur, who was an American and couldn't bear him, feeling the very essence of class superiority in that tone.

A few months later she showed an English illustrated to Miss Bennett.

"A picture of the girl Ilseboro is going to marry."

There was a pause while Miss Bennett read those romantic words: "A marriage has been arranged and will shortly take place between George Frederick Albert Reade, Marquis of Ilseboro,and—"

"She looks like a lady," said Miss Bennett.

"She looks like a rabbit," said Lydia. "Just think how Freddy will order her about!"

It was not in her nature to feel remorse for her well-considered actions, and she soon forgot that Ilseboro had ever existed, except for certain things she had learned from him—a way

7

of being silent while people explained to you you couldn't do something you intended to do, and then doing it instead of arguing about it, as had been her old habit; and an excellent manner with butlers too.

Her foot pressed gently on the accelerator, when the road became straight, holding the car now at forty miles. On either side of the road purple cabbages grew like a tufted carpet to the very edge of the macadam, without fences or hedges to protect them. There was enough mist in the autumn air to magnify the low hills along the Sound to an imposingly vague bulk, and to turn the cloudless sky to a threatening bluish gray. In every other direction the flat, fertile, sandy plains of Long Island stretched uninterruptedly.

It was really a beautiful afternoon—too beautiful to spend playing bridge in a stuffy room. It might be more sensible, she thought, to break up the party, kidnap Bobby and drive him over to sit on the edge of the water and watch the moon rise; only she rather feared the moon was over. Of course she was dining at the Leonard Piers' that evening, but it was a party eminently chuckable—that is to say, she was going to please them rather than herself. Anyhow, she would have Eleanor move the bridge table out on the terrace. Eleanor was so stupid about preferring to play indoors.

A minute figure, smaller than a man's hand, flashed into the little mirror at her left. Was it—no—yes? A bicycle policeman! Well, she would give him a little race for his stupidity in not recognizing her. She loved speed—it made her a little drunk. The needle swung to forty-five—to fifty, and hung there. She passed a governess cart full of children with a sound like "whist" as the wind rushed by. Now there was a straight road, and clear.

The miniature figure kept growing and growing until it seemed to fill the whole circle of the mirror. The sound of the motorcycle drowned the sound of her own car. A voice shouted "Stop!" almost in her ear. Turning her head slightly to the left, she saw a khaki figure was abreast of her. She slowed the car down and stopped it. A sunburned young face flushed with anger glared at her.

"Here, what do you think this is? A race track?"

Lydia did not answer, staring straight ahead of her. She was thinking that it was a foolish waste of taxpayers' money to keep changing the policemen. Just as you reached a satisfactory arrangement with one of them you found yourself confronted by another. She wasn't in the least alarmed, though he was scolding her roughly—scolding, to be candid, very much as her own father had done. She did not object to his words, but she hated the power

8

of the law behind them—hated the idea that she herself was not the final judge of the rate at which she should drive.

Now he was getting his summons ready. Glancing idly into her mirror, she saw far away, like a little moving picture, the governess cart come into view. She intended to settle the matter before those giggling, goggle-eyed children came abreast. She was a person in whom action followed easily and instantly from the decision to act. Most people, after making a decision, hesitate like a stream above a waterfall, and then plunging too quickly, end in foam and whirlpools. But Lydia's will, for good or evil, flowed with a steady current.

She looked down at the seat beside her for her mesh bag, opened it and found that Evans, who was a good deal of a goose, had forgotten to put her purse in it, although she knew bridge was to be played. Lydia looked up and saw that the officer of the law had followed her gesture with his eyes. She slipped Bobby's bracelet off her arm, and holding her hand well over the edge of the car dropped it on the road. She heard it tinkle on the hard surface.

"You dropped something," he said.

"No."

He swung a gaitered leg from the motorcycle and picked up the bracelet.

"Isn't this yours?"

She smiled very slightly and shook her head, once again in complete mastery of the situation.

"Whose is it then?"

"I think it must be yours," she answered with a sort of sweet contempt, and still looking him straight in the eye she leaned over and put her gear in first. He said nothing, and her car began to move forward. Presently she heard the sound of a motorcycle going in the opposite direction. She smiled to herself. There was always a way.

She found them waiting for her at Eleanor's, and she felt at once that the atmosphere was hostile; but when Lydia really liked people, and she really liked all the three who were waiting, she had command of a wonderfully friendly coöperative sort of gayety that was hard to resist.

She liked Eleanor Bellington better than any woman she knew. They had been friends since their school days. Eleanor had brains and a dry, bitter tongue, usually silent, and she wasn't the least bit afraid of Lydia. She was blond, plain, aristocratic, independent and some years Lydia's senior. Fearless in thought, she was conservative in conduct. All her activity was in the intellectual field, or else vicariously, through the activity of others. There were

9

always two or three interesting men, coming men, men of whom one said on speaking of them "You know, he's the man—" who seemed to be intimately woven into Eleanor's everyday life. A never-ending subject of discussion among Miss Bellington's friends was the exact emotional standing of these intimacies of Nellie's.

Lydia liked Tim Andrews too—a young man of universal friendships and no emotions; but most necessary of all to her enjoyment was Bobby Dorset, who came out to meet her, sauntering down the steps with his hands in his pockets. He looked exactly as a young man ought to look—physically fit, masculine. He was young—younger than his twenty-six years. There wasn't a line of any kind in his clean-shaven face, and the time had come—had almost come—when something ought to have been written there. The page was remaining blank too long. That was the only criticism possible of Bobby's appearance, and perhaps only an elderly critic would have thought of making it. Lydia certainly did not. When he smiled at her, showing his regular, handsome teeth, she thought he was the nicest-looking person she knew.

Just as she had expected, the bridge table was set inside the house, and while she was protesting and having it moved to the terrace she mentioned that she was late because she had had a fuss with Miss Bennett.

"Dear little Benny," said Andrews. "She's like a nice brown-eyed animal with gray fur, isn't she?"

"Tim always talks as if he were in love with Benny."

"She's so gentle, Lydia, and you are so ruthless with her," said Dorset.

"I have to be, Bobby," answered Lydia, and perhaps to no one else would she have stooped to offer an explanation. "She's gentle, but marvelously persistent. She gets her own way by slow infiltration. I wish you'd all tell me what to do. Benny is a person on whom what you say in a critical way makes no impression until you say it so as to hurt her feelings, and then it makes no impression because she's so taken up with her feelings being hurt. That's my problem with her."

"It's everybody's problem with everybody," replied Eleanor.

"She likes to ask her dull friends to the house when I'm there to entertain them."

"Entertain them with a blackjack," said Bobby.

"She had two prison reformers there to-day—old women with pear-shaped faces, and I had a perfectly horrid morning in town trying to get some rags to put on my back, and—Nell, will you tell me why you recommended Lurline to me? I never saw such atrocious clothes."

"I didn't recommend her," answered Nellie, unstampeded by the attack. "I told you that pale, pearl-like chorus girl dressed there, and your latent desire to dress like a chorus girl—"

"Oh, Lydia doesn't want to dress like a chorus girl!"

"Thank you, Bobby."

"She wants to dress like the savages in Aïda."

"In mauve maillots and chains?"

"In tiger skins and beads, and crouch through the jungle."

"I was so sulky I didn't give a cent to prison reform. Do you think prisons ought to be made too comfortable? I don't want to be cruel, but—"

"Well, it's something, my dear, that you don't want to be."

"You mean I am? That's what Benny says. But I'm not. Is this ten cents a point?"

Eleanor, who like many intellectuals found her excitement in fields where chance was eliminated, protested that ten cents a point was too high, but her objections were swept away by Lydia.

"Oh, no, Eleanor; play for beans if you want; but if you are going to gamble at all—"

Tim Andrews interrupted.

"My dear Lydia," he said, "I feel it only right to tell you that the Anti-Lydia Club was being organized when you arrived. Its membership consists of all those you have bullied, and its object is to oppose you in all small matters."

"Whether I'm right or not, Tim?"

"Everybody's worst when they're right," murmured Eleanor.

"We decided before you came that we all wished to play five cents a point," Tim continued firmly.

"All right," said Lydia briskly. "Only you know it bores me, and it bores Bobby, too, doesn't it, Bobby?"

"Not particularly," replied Dorset; "but I know if it bores you none of us will have a pleasant time."

Lydia smiled.

"Is that an insult or a tribute?"

Bobby smiled back at her.

"I think it's an insult, but you rather like it."

Half an hour later they were playing for ten cents a point.

CHAPTER II

Lydia had offered to drop Bobby at the railroad station on her way home, although she had to go a few miles out of her way to do it. He was going back to town. It was dark by the time they started. She liked the feeling of having him there tucked in beside her while she absolutely controlled his destiny for the next half hour. She liked even to take risks with his life, more precious to her at least for the time than any other, in the hope that he would protest, but he never did. He understood his Lydia.

After a few minutes she observed, "I suppose you know Eleanor has a new young man."

"Intensely interesting, or absolutely worth while?" he asked.

"Both, according to her. She's bringing him out at the Piers' this evening. She was just asking me to be nice to him."

"Like asking the boa constrictor to be nice to a newborn lamb, isn't it?"

"If I'm nice to her men it gives her a feeling of confidence in them."

"If you're nice to them you take them away from her."

"No, Bobby. It's a funny thing, but it isn't so easy as you think to get Eleanor's men away from her."

"Ah, you've tried?"

"She has a funny kind of hold on them. It's her brains. She has brains, and they appreciate it. I don't often want her men. They're apt to be so dreadful. Do you remember the biologist with the pearl buttons on his boots? This one is in politics—or something. He has a funny name—O'Bannon."

"Oh, yes—Dan O'Bannon."

"You know him?"

"I used to know him in college. Lord, he was a wild man in those days!" Bobby snickered reminiscently. "And now he's the local district attorney."

"What does a district attorney do, Bobby?"

"Why, he's a fellow elected by the county to prosecute—"

"Look here, Bobby, if the Emmonses ask you to spend this coming Sunday with them, go, because I'm going." She interrupted him because it was the kind of explanation that she had never been able to listen to. In fact she had so completely ceased to listen that she was unaware of having interrupted the answer to her own question, and Bobby did not care to bring the matter to her attention for fear her invitation to the Emmonses might be lost in

12

the subsequent scuffle. Besides he esteemed it his own fault. Most people who ask you a question like that really mean to say, "Would there be anything interesting to me in the answer to this question? If not, for goodness' sake don't answer it." So he gladly abandoned defining the duties of the district attorney and answered her more important statement.

"Of course I'll go, only they haven't asked me."

"They will—or else I won't go. You'll come out on Friday afternoon."

"I can't, Lydia, until Saturday."

"Now, Bobby, don't be absurd. Don't let that old man treat you like a slave."

Lydia's attitude to Bobby's work was a trifle confusing. She wished him to attain a commanding position in the financial world but had no patience with his industry when it interfered with her own plans. The attaining of any position at all seemed unlikely in Bobby's case. He was a clerk in the great banking house of Gordon & Co., a firm which in the course of a hundred and twenty-five years had built itself into the very financial existence of the country. In almost any part of the civilized globe to say you were with Gordon & Co. was a proud boast. But pride was all that a man of Bobby's type was likely to get out of it. Promotion was slow. Lydia talked of a junior partnership some day, but Bobby knew that partnerships in Gordon & Co. went to qualities more positively valuable than his. Sometimes he thought of leaving them, but he could not bear to give up the easy honor of the connection.

It was better to be a doorkeeper with Gordon & Co. than a partner with some ephemeral firm.

It amused him to hear her talk of Peter Gordon treating him like a slave. The dignified, middle-aged head of the firm, whose business was like an ancestral religion to him, hardly knew his clerks by sight.

"It isn't exactly servile to work half a day on Saturday," he said mildly.

"They'd respect you more if you asserted yourself. Do come on Friday, Bobby. I shall be so bored if you're not there."

He reflected that after all he would rather be dismissed by Gordon & Co. than by the young lady beside him.

"Dearest Lydia, how nice you can be when you want to—like all tyrants."

They had reached the small deserted wooden hut that served as a railroad station, and Lydia stopped the car.

"I suppose it's silly, but I wish you wouldn't say that—that I'm a tyrant," she said appealingly. "I don't want to be, only so often I know I know better what ought to be done. This afternoon, for instance, wasn't it much better for us all to play outside instead of in that stuffy little room of Eleanor's? Was that being a tyrant?"

"Yes, Lydia, it was; but I like it. All I ask is a little tyrant in my home."

She sighed so deeply that he leaned over and kissed her cool cheek.

"Good-by, my dear," he said.

The kiss did not go badly. He had done it as if, though not sure of success, he was not adventuring on absolutely untried ground.

"I think you'd better not do that, Bobby."

"Do you hate it?"

"Not particularly, only I don't want you to get dependent on it."

He laughed as he shut the car door. The light of the engine was visible above the low woods to their left.

"I'll take my chances on that," he said.

As she drove away she felt the injustice of the world. Everyone did ask your advice; they did want you to take an interest, but they complained when this interest led you to exert the slightest pressure on them to do what you saw was best. That was so illogical. You couldn't give a person advice that was any good unless you entered in and made their problem yours, and of course if you did that—only how few people except herself ever did it for their friends—then you were concerned, personally concerned that they should follow your advice. They were all content, too, she thought, when her tyranny worked out for their good. Bobby, for instance, had not complained of her having forced the Emmonses to ask him for Sunday. He thought that commendable. Perhaps the Emmonses hadn't. And yet how much better to be clear. She did not want to go and spend Sunday with anyone unless she could be sure of having someone to amuse her. Suppose she had gone there and found that like Benny they were using her to entertain some of their dull friends. That would have made her angry. She might have been disagreeable and broken up a friendship. This way it was safe.

She did not get home until half past seven, and she was dining at eight, fifteen minutes' drive away.

A pleasant smell of roses and wood smoke greeted her as she entered the house. She loved her house, with the broad shingles and classic pilasters of the front still untouched. Ten years ago her father had bought it—a nice old farmhouse with an ornamental band running round it below the eaves and a perfect little porch before the door. Since then she had been becoming more and more

14

attached to it as it became more and more the work of her own creation. She had added whatever she needed without much regard to the effect of the whole—a large paneled room, English as much as anything, an inner garden suggestive of a Spanish patio, a tiled Italian hall and a long servant's wing that was nothing at all.

She put her head in the dining room, where Miss Bennett in a stately tea gown was just beginning a solitary dinner.

"Hello, Benny! Have a good dinner. I forgot to tell you I'm going to the Emmonses for Sunday, so if you want to ask someone down to keep you company, do. I'm going to be late for dinner."

Miss Bennett smiled and nodded, recognizing this as a peace demonstration. Fourteen years had taught her that Lydia was not without generosity.

Fourteen years ago this coming winter the Thornes had entered Miss Bennett's life. Old Joe Thorne had come by appointment to her little New York apartment. The appointment had been made by a friend of Miss Bennett's—Miss Bennett's friends were always looking for something desirable for her in those days. Her family, who had been identified with New York for a hundred and fifty years, had gradually declined in fortune until the panic of 1893 had almost wiped out the little fortune of Adeline and her mother, the last of the family. Adeline had been brought up, not in luxury but in a comfortable, unalterable feminine idleness. She had always had all the clothes she needed to go about among the people she knew, and they were the people who had everything. The Bennetts had never kept a carriage, but they had never stinted themselves in cabs. The truth was they had never stinted themselves in anything that they really wanted. And Adeline, when she found herself alone in the world at thirty, with an income of only a few thousand, continued the family tradition of having what she wanted. She took a small apartment, which she contrived to make charming, and she lived nicely by the aid of her old French nurse, who came and cooked for her and dressed her and turned her out as perfectly as ever. She continued to dine out every night, and though nominally she spent her summers in New York as an economy, she was always on somebody's yacht or in somebody's country house. She paid any number of visits and enjoyed life more than most people.

Her friends, however, for she had the power of creating real attachments, were not so well satisfied. At first they were persuaded that Adeline would marry—it was so obviously the thing for Adeline to do—but she was neither designing nor romantic. She lacked both the reckless emotion which may lead one to marry badly and the cold-blooded determination to marry well.

She was just past forty the day Joe Thorne came. She could still see him as he entered in his blue overcoat with a velvet collar. A big powerful man with prominent eyes like Bismarck's, and a heavy dark brown mustache bulging over his upper lip. He did not expect to give much time to the interview. He had come to see if Miss Bennett would do to bring up his daughter, who at ten years was giving him trouble. He wanted her prepared for the social opportunities he intended her to have. It seemed strange to him that a person who lived as simply as Miss Bennett could really have these social opportunities in her control, but he had been advised by people whom he trusted that such was the fact, and he accepted it.

He was the son of a Kansas farmer, had left the farm as a boy and settled in a small town, and had learned the trade of bricklaying. By hard work he gradually amassed a few hundred dollars, and this he invested in a gravel bank just outside the town. It was the only gravel bank in the neighborhood and brought him a high return on the money. Then just as the gravel was exhausted the town began to spread in that direction, and Thorne was arranging to level his property and sell it in building lots, when a still more unexpected development took place. Oil was struck in the neighborhood, and beneath Thorne's gravel lay a well.

If Fate had intended him to be poor she should never have allowed him to make his first thousand dollars, for from the moment he had any surplus everything he touched did well. In one of his trips to the Louisiana oil district he met and married a local belle, a slim, pale girl with immense dark-circled black eyes and a skin like a gardenia. She followed him meekly about the country from oil wells to financial centers until after the birth of her daughter. Then she settled down in Kansas City and waited his rare visits. The only inconsiderate thing she had ever done to him was to die and leave him with an eight-year-old daughter.

For several stormy years he tried various solutions—foreign governesses who tried to marry him, American college girls who attempted to make him take his fair share of parental responsibility, an old cousin who had been a school teacher and dared to criticize his manner of life. At last his enlarging affairs brought him to New York and he heard of Miss Bennett. He heard of her through Wiley, his lawyer. Wiley, a man in the forties, then attaining preëminence at the bar in New York, had been thought by many people to be an ideal husband for Adeline. They were old friends. He admired her, wished her well, and thought of her instantly when his new client applied to him for help.

The minute Thorne saw Miss Bennett he saw that she would do perfectly. He made her the offer of a good salary. He couldn't

16

believe that she would refuse it. She could hardly believe it herself, for she was unaccustomed to setting up her will against anyone's least of all against a man like Joe Thorne, who had successfully battled his way up against the will of the world. The contest went on for weeks and weeks. Poor Miss Bennett kept consulting her friends, almost agreeing to go when she saw Thorne, and then telephoning him that she had changed her mind, and bringing him round to her apartment—which was just what she didn't want—to argue her into it again.

Some of her friends opposed her going to the house of a widower whose reputation in regard to women was not spotless. Others thought—though they did not say—that if she went, and succeeded in marrying him, she would be doing better than she had any right to expect. Perhaps if Miss Bennett could have fallen in love with Lydia she might have yielded, but even at ten, Lydia, a black-eyed determined little person, inspired fear more than love.

Poor Adeline grew pale and thin over the struggle. At last she decided, after due consultation with friends, to end the matter by being a little bit rude, by telling Thorne that she just didn't like the whole prospect; that she preferred her own little place and her own little life.

"Like it—like this cramped little place?" he said, looking about at the sunshine and chintz and potted daisies of her cherished home. "But I'd make you comfortable, give you what you ought to have—Europe, your friends, your carriage, everything."

He went on to argue with her that she was wrong, utterly wrong to like her own life. Her last card didn't win. She yielded at last for no better reason than that her powers of resistance were exhausted.

Thorne was then living in a house on a corner of upper Fifth Avenue, with a pale-pink brocade ballroom running across the front and taking all the morning sunshine, and a living room and library at the back so dark that you couldn't read in it at mid-day, with marble stairs and huge fire-places that didn't draw—a terrible house. Some years later, under Miss Bennett's influence, he had bought the more modest house in the Seventies where Lydia now spent her winters. But it was to the Fifth Avenue house that Miss Bennett came, and found herself plunged into one of the most desperate struggles in the world. Thorne, whose continuous interest was given to business, attempted to rule Lydia in crises—by scenes, scenes of a violence that Miss Bennett had never seen equaled. As it turned out, her coming weakened Thorne's power; not that she wasn't usually on his side—she was—but she was an audience, and

17

Thorne had some sense of shame before an audience, while Lydia had none at all.

Many a time she had seen him box Lydia's ears and, mild as she was, had been glad to see him do it. But it was his violence that undid him. It was then that Lydia became suddenly dignified and, unbroken, contrived to make him appear like a brute.

There is nothing really more unbreakable than a child who considers neither her physical well-being nor public opinion. An older person, however violent, has learned that he must consider such questions, and it is a weakness in a campaign of violence to consider anything but the desired end.

And on the whole Thorne lost. He could make Lydia do or refrain from doing specific acts—at least he could when he was at home. He had not permitted her at ten to keep her great Danes nor at thirteen to drive a high-stepping hackney in a red-wheeled cart which she ordered for herself without consultation with anyone.

The evening after that struggle was over he had asked Miss Bennett to marry him. She knew why he did it. Lydia in the course of the row had referred to her as a paid companion. He had long been considering it as a sensible arrangement, particularly in case of his death. Miss Bennett refused him. She tried to think that she had been tempted by his offer, but she was not. To her he seemed a violent man who had been a bricklayer, and she always breathed a sigh of relief when he was out of the house. She was glad that he did not press the point, but in after years it was a solid comfort to her to remember that she might have been Lydia's stepmother if she had chosen.

But it was in the long-drawn-out contest that Thorne failed. He could not make Lydia keep governesses that she didn't like. Her method was simple—she made their lives so disagreeable that nothing could make them stay. He never succeeded in getting her to boarding school, though he and Miss Bennett, after a long conference, decided that that was the thing to do. But that failure was partly due to his failing health.

That was their last great struggle. He died in 1912. In his will he left Miss Bennett ten thousand a year, with the request that she stay with his daughter until her marriage. It touched Miss Bennett that he should have seen that she could not have stayed if she had been dependent on Lydia's capricious will. It was this that made her position possible—the fact that they both knew she could go in an instant if she wanted; not that she ever doubted that Lydia was sincerely attached to her.

18

CHAPTER III

When Lydia ran upstairs to dress everything was waiting for her—the lights lit, the fires crackling, her bath drawn, her underclothes and stockings folded on a chair, her green-and-gold dress spread out upon the bed, her narrow gold slippers standing exactly parallel on the floor beside it, and in the midst Evans, like a priestess waiting to serve the altar of a goddess, was standing with her eyes on the clock.

Lydia snatched off her hat, rumpled her hair with both hands as Evans began to undo her blouse. She unfastened the cuff, and then looked up with pale startled eyes.

"Your bracelet, miss?"

"Bracelet?" For a second Lydia had really forgotten it.

"The little diamond bracelet. You were wearing it this afternoon."

Something panic-stricken and excited in the girl's tone annoyed Lydia.

"I must have dropped it," she said.

The maid gave a little cry as if she herself had suffered a loss.

"Oh, to lose a valuable bracelet like that!"

"If I don't mind I don't see why you should, Evans."

Evans began unhooking her skirt in silence.

Twenty minutes later she was being driven rapidly toward the Piers'. These minutes were among the most contemplative of her life, shut in for a few seconds alone without possibility of interruption. Now as she leaned back she thought how lonely her life was—always facing criticism alone. Was she a bully, as Ilseboro had said? Perhaps she was hard. But then how could you get things done if you were soft? There was Benny. Benny, with many excellent abilities, was soft, and look where she was—a paid companion at fifty-five. Lydia suspected that ten years before her father had wanted to marry Benny, and Benny had refused. Lydia thought she knew why—because Benny thought old Joe Thorne a vulgar man whom she didn't love. Very high-minded, of course, and yet wasn't there a sort of weakness in not taking your chance and putting through a thing like that? Wouldn't Benny be more a person from every point of view if she had decided to marry the old man for his money? If she had she'd have been his widow now, and Lydia a dependent step-daughter. How she would have hated that!

The Piers had built a perfect French château, and had been successful in changing the scrubby woods into gardens and terraces and groves. Lydia stepped out of the car and paused on the wide marble steps, wrapping her cloak about her with straight arms, as an Indian wraps his blanket about him. She turned her head slightly at her chauffeur's inquiry as to the hour of her return.

"Oh," she said, "eight—ten—bridge. Come back at eleven."

The mirrors in the Piers' dressing room were flattering as she dropped her cloak with one swift motion into the hands of the waiting servant and saw a reflection of her slim gold-and-green figure with the emerald band across her forehead.

She saw at a glance on entering the drawing-room that it wasn't a very good party—only eight, and nothing much in the line of bridge players. She listened temperately to Fanny Piers' explanation that four people had given out since six o'clock. She nodded, admitting the excuse and reserving the opinion that if the Piers gave better parties people wouldn't chuck them so often.

She looked about. There was Tim Andrews again. Well, she could always amuse herself well enough with Tim. May Swayne—a soft blond creature whom Lydia had known for many years and ignored. Indeed, May was as little aware of Lydia's methods as a mole of a thunderstorm. Then there was Hamilton Gore, the lean home wrecker of a former generation, not bad—a little elderly, a little too epigrammatic for the taste of this day; but still, once a home wrecker always a home wrecker. He was still stimulating. The last time she had talked to him he had called her a sleek black panther. That always pleases, of course. Since then Fanny Piers, a notable mischief-maker, had repeated something else he said. He had called her a futile barbarian. She disliked the "futile." She would take it up with him; that would amuse her if everything else failed. She would say, "Hello, Mr. Gore! I suppose you hardly expected to meet a barbarian at dinner—especially a futile one." It would make Fanny wretched, but then if Fanny would repeat things she must expect to get into trouble.

And then, of course, there was Eleanor's new best bet—the intensely interesting and absolutely worthwhile young man. Lydia looked about, and there he was. Dear me, she thought, he certainly was interesting and worth while, but not quite from the point of view Eleanor had suggested—public service and political power. He was very nice looking, tall and heavy in the shoulders. He was turned three-quarters from her as she made her diagnosis. She could see little more than his mere size, the dark healthy brown of a sunburned Anglo-Saxon skin, and the deep point at the back of his neck where short thick hair grew in a deep point. Eleanor, looking small beside him, was staring idly before her, not attempting to show him off. There was nothing cheap about Eleanor. She spoke to

20

him now, preparing to introduce him to her friend. Lydia saw him turn, and their eyes met—the queerest eyes she had ever seen. She found herself staring into them longer than good manners allowed; not that Lydia cared much about good manners, but she did not wish to give the man the idea she had fallen in love with him at first sight; only it just happened that she had never seen eyes before that flared like torches, grew dark and light and small and large like a cat's, only they weren't the color of a cat's, being gray—a pure light gray in contrast with his dark hair and skin. There was a contrast in expression too. They were a little mad, at least fanatical, whereas his mouth was controlled and legal and humorus. What was it Bobby had said about him in college—a wild man? She could well believe it. During these few seconds Eleanor was introducing him, and she was casting about for something to say to him. That was the trouble with meeting new people—it was so much easier to chatter to old friends. Benny said that was provincial. She made a great effort.

"How are you?"—this quite in the Ilseboro manner. "Are you staying near here?"

You might have counted one-two before he betrayed the least sign of having heard her. Then he said, "Yes, I live about ten miles from here."

"Oh, of course! You're a judge or something like that, aren't you?"

Was the man a little deaf?

"Something like that."

She noted that trick of pausing a second or two before answering. Ilseboro had had it too. It was rather effective in a way. It made the other person wonder if what he had said was foolish. He wasn't deaf a bit—quite the contrary.

"Aren't you going to tell me what you are?" she said.

He shook his head gravely. Then her eye fell on Gore standing at her elbow and she couldn't resist the temptation. She turned her back on Eleanor's discovery.

"Hullo, Mr. Gore! Did you expect to meet a barbarian at dinner—especially a futile one?"

Gore, unabashed, took the whole room in.

"Now," he said in his high-pitched voice, "could anything be more barbarous than that attack? Oh, yes, I said it; and what's worse, I think it, my dear young lady—I think it!"

She turned back to O'Bannon.

"Would you think I was a barbarian?"

"Certainly not a futile one," he answered.

They went in to dinner. It was a fixed principle of Fanny Piers' life to put her women friends next to their own young men, so that

Eleanor found herself next to O'Bannon at dinner. He was on his hostess' right, Gore on her left, then Lydia and Tim and May and Piers, and Eleanor again. The arrangement suited Lydia very well. She went on baiting Gore. It suited Eleanor even better. She had known Noel Piers far too long to waste any time talking to him, and as this was the arrangement he preferred, they were almost friends. This left her free to talk to O'Bannon. Her native ability, joined to her personal interest in him, made her familiar with every aspect of his work. He talked shop to her and loved it. He was telling her of a case in which labor unions, with whose aims he himself as an individual was in sympathy, had made themselves amenable to the law. That was one of the penalties of a position like his. Piers caught a few words and leaned over.

"Well, I'm pretty liberal," he said—that well-known opening of the reactionary—"but I'm not in favor of labor."

"Not even for others, Noel," said Eleanor, who did not want to be interrupted.

"I mean labor unions," replied Piers, who, though not without humor in its proper place, had too much difficulty in expressing an idea to turn aside to laugh about it. "I hope you'll be firm with those fellows, O'Bannon. I hope you're not a socialist like Eleanor."

Piers had used the word "socialist" as a hate word, and expected to hear O'Bannon repudiate the suggestion as an insult. Instead he denied it as a fact.

"No," he said, "I'm not a socialist. I think you'll find lawyers conservative as a general thing. I believe in my platform—the equal administration of the present laws. That's radical enough—for the present."

Piers gave a slight snort. Everyone, he said, believed in that.

"I don't find they do—it isn't my experience," answered O'Bannon. "Some fellows broke up a socialist meeting the other evening in New York, and no one was punished, although not only were people injured, but even property was damaged." Eleanor was the only person who caught the "even." "You know very well that if the socialists broke in on a meeting of well-to-do citizens they would be sent up the river."

Piers stared at his guest with his round, bloodshot eyes. He was a sincere man, and stupid. He reached his conclusions by processes which had nothing to do with thought, and when someone talked like this—attacking his belief that it was wrong to break up his meetings and right to break up the other man's—he felt as he did at a conjurer's performance: that it was all very clever, but a sensible person knew it was a trick, even though he could not explain how it was done.

22

"I'm not much good at an argument," he said, "but I know what's right. I know what the country needs, and if you show favoritism to these disloyal fellows I shall vote against you next time, I tell you frankly."

Lydia, hearing by the tones that the conversation across the table promised more vitality than her waning game with Gore about the barbarian epithet, dropped her own sentence and answered, "No one really believes in equality who's on top. I believe in special privilege."

O'Bannon, who had been contemptuously annoyed with Piers, was amused at Lydia's frankness as she bent her head to look at him under the candle shades and the light gleamed in her eyes and flashed on the emeralds on her forehead. Beauty, after all, is the greatest special privilege of all.

"That's what I said," he returned. "No one honestly believes in my platform—the equal administration of the present laws."

"I do," said Piers. "I do—everyone does."

O'Bannon glanced at him, and deciding that it wasn't worth while to take him round the circle again let the sentence drop.

"Do you believe in it yourself, Mr. O'Bannon?" asked Lydia, and she stretched out a slim young arm and moved the candle so that she could look straight at him or he at her. "I mean, if you caught some friend smuggling—me, for example—would you be as implacable as if you caught my dressmaker?"

"More so; you would have less excuse."

She laughed and shook her head.

"You know in your heart it never works like that."

"Unfortunately," he answered, "my office does not take me into Federal customs, or you might find I was right."

"The administration of the customs of the United States," Piers began, but his wife interrupted.

"Don't explain it, there's a dear," she said, and oddly enough he didn't.

Lydia was delighted with O'Bannon's challenging tone.

"I wish you were," she said, "because I know you would turn out to be just like everyone else. Or even if you are a superman, Mr. O'Bannon, you couldn't be sure all your underlings were equally noble."

"What you mean is that you habitually bribe customs inspectors."

"No," said Lydia, as one surprised at her own moderation—"no, I don't, for I never much mind paying duty; but if I did mind—well, I must own I have bribed other officers of the law with very satisfactory results."

23

O'Bannon, looking at her under the shades, thought—and perhaps conveyed his thought to her—that she could bribe him very easily with something more desirable than gold. It was Gore who began carefully to point out to her the risk run by the taker of the bribe.

"You did not think of him, my dear young lady."

"Yes, I did," answered Lydia. "He wanted the money and I wanted the freedom. It was nice for both of us." She glanced at O'Bannon, who was talking to Mrs. Piers as if Lydia didn't exist. She felt no hesitation in interrupting.

"You couldn't put me in prison for that, could you, Mr. O'Bannon?"

"No, I'm afraid not," said O'Bannon, and turned back to Fanny Piers.

After dinner she told Eleanor in strict confidence the story of the bicycle policeman, and made her promise not to tell O'Bannon.

"I shouldn't dream of telling anyone," said Eleanor with her humorous lift of the eyebrows. "I think it's a perfectly disgusting story and represents you at your worst."

When they sat down to bridge Lydia drew O'Bannon, and whatever antagonism had flashed out between them at dinner disappeared in a perfectly adjusted partnership. They found they played very much the same sort of game; they understood one another's makes and leads, and knew as if by magic the cards that the other held. It seemed as if they could not mistake each other. They were both courageous players, ready to take a chance, without overbidding. They knew when to be silent, and, with an occasional bad hand, to wait. But the bad hands were few. They had the luck not only of holding high cards but of holding cards which invariably supported each other. Their eyes met when they had triumphantly doubled their opponents' bids; they smiled at each other when they had won a slam by a subtle finesse or by patiently forcing discards. Their winnings were large. Lydia seemed as steady as a rock—not a trace of excitement in her look.

O'Bannon thought, after midnight when he was totaling the score, "I could make a terrible fool of myself about this girl."

When they were leaving he found himself standing on the steps beside her. The footman had run down the drive to see why her chauffeur, after a wait of more than an hour, wasn't bringing her car round. O'Bannon, who was driving himself in an open car, came out, turning up the collar of his overcoat, and found himself alone with her in the pale light of the waning moon, which gave, as the waning moon always does, the effect of being a strange, unfamiliar celestial visitor.

O'Bannon, like so many strict supporters of law, was subject to invasions of lawless impulses. He thought now how easy it would be to run off with a girl like this one and teach her that civilization was not such a complete protection as she thought it. What an outcry she would make, and yet perhaps she wouldn't really object! He had a theory that men and women were more susceptible to emotion in the first minutes of their meeting than at any subsequent time—at least in such first meetings as this.

She was standing wrapping her black-and-silver cloak about her with that straight-armed Indian pose.

"It's a queer light, isn't it?" she said.

He agreed. Something certainly was queer—the greenish silver light on the withered leaves or the mist like a frothy flood on the lawn. Just as she spoke two brighter lights shone through the mist—her car coming up the drive with the footman standing on the step.

"Is that yours?" he asked.

She nodded, knowing that he was watching her.

"Why don't you send it away," he went on very quietly, "and let me drive you home? This is no night for a closed car."

He hardly knew whether he had a plan or not, but his pulses beat more quickly as she walked down the steps without answering him. He did not know whether she was going to get into her car and drive away or give orders to the man to go home without her. Then he saw that the footman was closing the door on an empty car and the chauffeur releasing his brake. When she came up the steps he was looking at the moon.

"I never get used to its waning," he said, as if he had been thinking of nothing else.

She liked that—his not commenting in any way on her accepting an invitation not entirely conventional from a stranger. Perhaps he did not know that it wasn't. Oh, if he could only keep on like that—maintaining that remote impersonality until she herself wanted him to be different! But if he wrapped the lap robe about her with too lingering an arm, or else, flying to the other extreme, began to be friendly and chatty, pretending that there was nothing extraordinary in two strangers being alone like this in a sleeping, moonlit world—

He did neither. When he brought the car to the steps the lap robe was folded back on the seat so that she could wrap it about her own knees. She did so with an exclamation. The mist clung in minute drops to its rough surface.

"It's wet," she said.

He did not answer—did not speak even, when as they left the

25

Piers' place it became necessary to choose their road. He chose without consultation.

"But do you know where I live?" she asked.

"Be content for once to be a passenger," he replied.

The answer had the good fortune to please. She leaned back, clasping her hands in her lap, relaxing all her muscles.

On the highroad she was less aware of the moon, for the headlights made the mist visible like a wall about them. She felt as if she were running through a new element and could detect nothing outside the car. She was detached from all previous experience, content to be, as he had said, for once a passenger. This was a new sensation. She remembered what Ilseboro had said about her being a bully. Well, she'd try the other thing to-night. She only hoped it wouldn't end in some sort of a scene. She glanced up at her companion's profile. It looked quiet enough, but she decided that she had better not go on much longer without making him speak. Her ear was well attuned to human vibrations, and if there were a certain low tremor in his voice—well, then it would be better to go straight home.

"This is rather extraordinary, isn't it?" she said. This might be interpreted in a number of ways.

"Yes, it is," he said, exactly matching her tone.

She tried him again.

"Did you enjoy the evening?" It seemed almost certain that he would answer tenderly, "I'm enjoying this part of it."

"It was good bridge," he said.

That sounded all right, she thought. His voice was as cool as her own. She could let things go and give herself up to enjoying the night and the moon and the motion and the damp air on her face and arms. She felt utterly at peace. Presently he turned from the highroad down a lane so untraveled that the low branches came swishing into her lap; they came out on a headland overlooking the Sound. Over the water the mist was only a thickening of the atmosphere which made the lights of a city across the water look like globes of yellow light in contrast to the clear red and white of a lighthouse in the foreground. He leaned forward and turned off the engine and lights.

Lydia found that she was trembling a little, which seemed strange, for she felt unemotional and still. And then all of a sudden she recognized that she was really waiting—waiting to feel her cheek against his rough frieze coat and his lips against hers. It was not exactly that she wanted it, but that it was inevitable—simple—not her choice—something that must be. This was an experience that she had never had before. In the silence she felt their mutual understanding rising like a tide. She had never felt so at one with any human being as with this stranger.

Suddenly he moved—but not toward her. She saw with astonishment that he was turning the switch, touching the self starter, and the next instant backing the car out. The divine moment was gone. She would never forgive him.

They drove back in silence, except for her occasional directions about the road. Her jaw was set like a little vise. Never again, she was saying to herself, would she allow herself to be a passenger. Hereafter she would control. It didn't matter what happened to you, if you were master of your own emotions. She remembered once that the husband of a friend of hers had caught her in his arms in the anteroom of a box at the opera during the darkness of a Wagnerian performance. She had felt like frozen steel—so sure of herself that she hardly hated the man—she felt more inclined to laugh at him. But this man who hadn't touched her, left her feeling outraged, humiliated—because she had wanted him to kiss her, to crush her to him—

They were at her door. She stepped out on the broad flat stones, under the trellis on which the grapevines grew so thickly that not even the flood of moonlight could penetrate the thick mass of verdure. The air was full of the smell of grapes. She knew he was following her. Suddenly she felt his hand, firm and confident on her shoulder, stopping her, turning her round. She did not resist him—she felt neither resistant nor acquiescent—only that it was all inevitable. He took her head in his two hands, looking in the dark and half drawing her to him, half bending down he pressed his lips hard against hers. She felt herself held closely in his arms; her will dissolved, her head drooped against him.

Then inside the house the steps of the faithful Morson could be heard. He must have been waiting for the sound of an approaching motor. The door opened—letting a great patch of yellow lamp light fall on the misty moonlight. Morson peered out; for a moment he thought he must have been mistaken; there appeared to be no one there. Then his young mistress, very erect, stepped out from the shadow. A tall gentleman, a stranger to Morson, said in a voice noticeably low and vibrant:

"At four to-morrow."

There was a pause. Morson holding the door open thought at first that Miss Thorne had not heard, and then she shocked him by her answer.

"No, don't come," she said. "I don't want you to come." She walked into the house, and indicated that he might shut the door. As he bolted it he could hear the motor moving away down the drive.

Turning from the door, he saw Miss Thorne standing still in the middle of the hall, as if she too were listening to the lessening drum of the engine. There was a long pause, and then Morson said:

"Shall I put out the lights, Miss?"

She nodded and went slowly upstairs, like a person in a trance.

She seemed hardly aware of Evans waiting to undress her, but stood still in her bedroom, as she had stood in the hall, staring blankly in front of her. Evans took her cloak from her shoulder.

"It's quite wet, Miss," she said, "as if it had been dipped in the sea and your hair, too."

Miss Thorne did not come to life, until in unhooking her dress Evans touched her with cold fingers. Then she started, exclaiming:

"What is the matter with you, Evans," she cried. "Do go and put your hands in hot water before you touch me. Your fingers are like ice."

The girl murmured that she had been upset since the loss of the bracelet—she felt responsible for Miss Thorne's jewels.

Lydia flung down the roll of bills and cheques that represented her evening's winnings. "I could buy myself another with what I've won to-night. Don't worry about it." The idea occurred to her that she would buy herself a sort of memento mori, something to remind her not to be a weak craven female thing again—nestling against men's shoulders like May Swayne.

Evans did not answer, but gathered up the money and the jewels and carried them into the dressing room to lock them in the safe.

CHAPTER IV

Lydia would have been displeased to know how little her curt refusal affected the emotional state of the man driving away from her door. It was the deed rather than the word that he remembered—the fact that he had held a beautiful and eventually unresisting woman in his arms that occupied his attention on his way home.

He found his mother sitting up—not for him. It was many years since Mrs. O'Bannon had gone to bed before two o'clock. She was a large woman, massive rather than fat. She was sitting by the fire in her bedroom, wrapped in a warm, loose white dressing gown, as white as her hair and smooth pale skin. Her eyes retained their deep darkness. Evidently Dan's gray eyes had come from his father's Irish ancestry.

It was only the other day—after he was grown up—that O'Bannon had ceased to be afraid of his mother. She was a woman passionately religious, mentally vigorous and singularly unjust, or at least inconsistent. It was this quality that made her so confusing and, to her subordinates, alarming. She would have gone to the stake—gone with a certain bitter amusement at the folly of her destroyers—for her belief in the right; but her affections could entirely sweep away these beliefs and leave her furiously supporting those she loved against all moral principles. Her son had first noticed that trait when she sent him away to boarding school. His mother—his father had died when he was seven—was a most relentless disciplinarian as long as a question of duty lay between him and her; but let an outsider interfere, and she was always on his side. She frequently defended him against the school authorities, and even, it seemed to him, encouraged him in rebellion. In her old age most of her strong passions had died away and left only her God and her son. Perhaps it was a trace of this persecutory religion in her that made Dan accept his present office.

She looked up like a sibyl from the great volume she was reading.

"You're late, my son."

"I've been gambling, mother."

He said it very casually, but it was the last remnant of his fear that made him mention particularly those of his actions of which he knew she would disapprove. In old times he had been a notable poker player, but had abandoned it on his election as district attorney. Her brow contracted.

29

"You should not do such things—in your position."

"My dear mother, haven't you yet grasped that there is a touch of the criminal in all criminal prosecutors? That's what draws us to the job."

She wouldn't listen to any such theory.

"Have you lost a great deal of money?" she asked severely.

"Not enough to turn us out of the old home," he smiled. "I won something under four hundred dollars."

Her brow cleared. She liked her son to be successful, preëminent in anything—right or wrong—which he undertook.

"You made a mistake to get mixed up with people like that," she said. She knew where he had been dining.

"I can't be said to have got mixed up with them. The only one I expressed any wish to see again slammed the door in my face."

The next instant he wished he had not spoken. He hoped his mother had not noticed what he said. She remained silent, but she had understood perfectly, and he had made for Lydia an implacable enemy. A woman who slammed the door in the face of Dan was deserving of hell-fire, in Mrs. O'Bannon's opinion. She did not ask who it was, because she knew that in the course of everyday life together secrets between two people are impossible and the name would come out.

After an almost sleepless night he woke in the morning with the zest of living extraordinarily renewed within him. Every detail in the pattern of life delighted him, from the smell of coffee floating up from the kitchen on the still cold of the November morning to the sight from his window of the village children in knit caps and sweaters hurrying to school—tall, lanky, competent girls bustling their little brothers along, and inattentive boys hoisting small sisters up the school steps by their arms. Life was certainly great fun, not because there were lovely women to be held in your arms, but because when young and vigorous you can bully life into being what you want it to be. And yet, good heavens, what a girl! At four that very afternoon he would see her again.

He was in court all the morning. The courthouse, which if it had been smaller would have looked like a mausoleum in a cemetery, and if it had been larger would have looked like the Madeleine, was set back from the main street. The case he was prosecuting—a case of criminal negligence against a young driver of a delivery wagon who had run over and injured a prominent citizen—went well; that is to say, O'Bannon obtained a conviction. It had been one of those cases clear to the layman, for the young man was notoriously careless; but difficult, as lawyers tell you criminal-negligence cases are, from the legal point of view.

30

O'Bannon came out of court very well satisfied both with himself and the jury and drove straight to the Thorne house. The smell of the grapes started his pulses beating. Morson came to the door. No, Miss Thorne was not at home.

"Did she leave any message for me?" said O'Bannon.

"Nothing, sir, except that she is not at home."

He eyed Morson, feeling that he would be within his masculine rights if he swept him out of the way and went on into the house; but tamely enough he turned and drove away. His feelings, however, were not tame. He was furious against her. How did she dare behave like this—driving about the country at midnight, gambling, letting him kiss her, and then ordering her door slammed in his face as if he were a book agent? Civilization gave such women too much protection. Perhaps the men she was accustomed to associating with put up with that kind of treatment, but not he. He'd see her again if he wanted to—yes, if he had to hold up her car on the highroad.

He thought with approval of Eleanor, a woman who played no tricks with you but left you cool and braced like a cold shower on a hot day. Yet he found that that afternoon he did not want to see Eleanor. He drove on and on, steeping himself in the bitterness of his resentment.

At dinner his mother noticed his abstraction and feared an important case was going wrong. Afterwards, supposing he wanted to think out some tangle of the law, she left him alone—not meditating, but seething.

The next morning at half past eight he was in his office. The district attorney's office was in an old brick block opposite the courthouse. It occupied the second story over Mr. Wooley's hardware shop. As he went in he saw Alma Wooley, the fragile blond daughter of his landlord, slipping in a little late for her duties as assistant in the shop. She was wrapped in a light-blue cloak the color of her transparent turquoise-blue eyes. She gave O'Bannon a pretty little sketch of a smile. She thought his position a great one, and his age extreme—anyone over thirty was ancient in her eyes. She was profoundly grateful to him, for he had given her fiancé a position on the police force and made their marriage a possibility at least.

"How are things, Alma?" he said.

"Simply wonderful, thanks to you, Mr. O'Bannon," she answered.

He went upstairs thinking kindly of all gentle blond women. In the office he found his assistant, Foster, the son of the local high-school teacher, a keen-minded ambitious boy of twenty-two.

31

"Oh," said Foster, "the sheriff's been telephoning for you. He's at the Thornes'."

O'Bannon felt as if his ears had deceived him.

"Where?" he asked sternly.

"At the Thornes' house—you know, there's a Miss Thorne who lives there—the daughter of old Joe S. Thorne." Then, seeing the blank look on his chief's face, Foster explained further. "It seems there was a jewel robbery there last night—a million dollars' worth, the sheriff says." He smiled, for the sheriff was a well-known exaggerator, but he met no answering smile. "They've been telephoning for you to come over."

"Who has?" said O'Bannon.

Foster thought him unusually slow of understanding this morning, and answered patiently, "Miss Thorne has. There's been a robbery there."

The district attorney was not slow in action.

"I'll go right over," he said, and left the office.

There were some advantages in holding public office. You could be sent for in your official capacity—and stick to it, by heaven!

This time he asked no questions at the door, but entered.

Morson said timidly, "Who shall I say, sir?"

"Say the district attorney."

Morson led the way to the drawing-room and threw open the door.

"The district attorney," he announced, making it sound like a title of nobility, and O'Bannon and Lydia stood face to face again— or rather he stood. She, leaning back in her chair, nodded an adequate enough greeting to a public servant in the performance of his duty. They were not alone—a slim gray-haired lady, Miss Bennett, was named.

"I understood at my office you had sent for me," said he.

"I?" There was something wondering in her tone. "Oh, yes, the sheriff, I believe, wanted you to come. All my jewels were stolen last night. He seemed to think you might be able to do something about it." Her tone indicated that she did not share the sheriff's optimism. Miss Bennett, with a long habit of counteracting Lydia's manners, broke in.

"So kind of you to come yourself, Mr. O'Bannon."

"It's my job to come."

"Yes, of course. I think I know your mother." She was very cordial, partly because she felt something hostile in the air, partly because she thought him an attractive-looking young man. "She's so helpful in the village improvement, only we're all just a little afraid of her. Aren't you just a little afraid of her yourself?"

32

"Very much," he answered gravely.

Miss Bennett wished he wouldn't just stare at her with those queer eyes of his—a little crazy, she thought. She liked people to smile at her when they spoke. She went on, "Not but what we work all the better for her because we are a little afraid—"

Lydia interrupted.

"Mr. O'Bannon hasn't come to pay us a social visit, Benny," she said, and this time there was something unmistakably insolent in her tone.

O'Bannon decided to settle this whole question on the instant. He turned to Miss Bennett and said firmly, "I should like to speak to Miss Thorne alone."

"Of course," said Miss Bennett, already on her way to the door, which O'Bannon opened for her.

"No, Benny, Benny!" called Lydia, but O'Bannon had shut the door and leaned his shoulders against it.

"Listen to me!" he said. "You must be civil to me—that is, if you want me to stay here and try to get your jewels back."

Lydia wouldn't look at him.

"And what guaranty have I that if you do stay you can do anything about it?"

"I think I can get them, and I can assure you the sheriff can't." There was a long pause. "Well?" he said.

"Well what?" said Lydia, who hadn't been able to think what she was going to do.

"Will you be civil, or shall I go?"

"I thought you just said it was your duty to stay."

"Make up your mind, please, which shall it be?"

Lydia longed to tell him to go, but she did want to get her jewels back, particularly as she was setting out for the Emmonses' in a few minutes, and it would save a lot of trouble to have everything arranged before she left. She thought it over deliberately, and looking up saw that he was amused at her cold-blooded hesitation. Seeing him smile, she found to her surprise that suddenly she smiled back at him. It was not what she had intended.

"Well," she thought, "let him think he's getting the best of me. As a matter of fact, I'm using him."

She hoped he would be content with the smile, but, no, he insisted on the spoken word. She was forced to say definitely that she would be civil. She carried it off, in her own mind at least, by saying it as if it were a childish game he was playing. Having received the assurance, he moved from the door and stood opposite her, leaning on the back of a chair.

"Now tell me what happened?" he said.

33

She told him how she had been waked up just before dawn by the sound of someone moving in her dressing room. At first she had thought it was a window, or a curtain blowing, until she had seen a fine streak of light under the door. Then she had sprung up—to find herself locked in. She had rung her bells, pounded on the door—finally succeeded in rousing the household. The dressing room was empty, but her safe had been opened—her jewels and about five hundred dollars gone—her recent winnings at bridge.

"You've had good luck lately?" he asked.

"Good partners," she answered with one of her illuminating smiles.

She'd gone all over the house after that. Alone? No. Morson had tagged on. Morson was afraid of burglars, having had experience with them in some former place. Besides, she always had a revolver. Oh, yes, she knew how to shoot! She'd gone over the whole house—there wasn't a lock undone.

He questioned her about the servants. Suspicion seemed to point to Evans, who had the run of the safe and might so easily have failed to lock it in the evening when she had put her mistress to bed. Lydia demurred at the idea of Evans' guilt. The girl had been with her for five years.

"I don't really think she has the courage to steal," she said.

"Do you know the circumstances of her life? Anything to make her feel in special need of money just now?" he inquired.

Lydia shook her head.

"I never see how servants spend their wages anyhow," she said. "But what makes me feel quite sure it isn't Evans is that I'm sure she would have confessed to me when I questioned her. Instead of that she's been packing my things for me just as usual."

O'Bannon cut the interview short by announcing that he'd see the sheriff. Lydia had expected—"dreaded" was her own word—that he would say something about the incidents of their last meeting. But he didn't. He left the room, saying as he went: "You'll wait here until I've had a talk with the girl."

His tone had a rising inflection of a question in it, but to Lydia it sounded like an order. She had had every intention of waiting, but now she began to contemplate the possibility of leaving at once. The car was at the door and her bags were on the car. How it would annoy him, she thought, if when he came back, instead of finding her patiently waiting to be civil, he learned that she had motored away, as much as to say: "It's your duty as an officer of the law to find my jewels, but it isn't my duty to be grateful to you."

Presently Miss Bennett and the sheriff came in together, talking—at least the sheriff was talking.

34

"It looks like it was her all right," he was saying, "and if so he'll get a confession out of her. That's why I sent for him. He's a great feller for getting folks to confess." Then with natural courtesy he turned to Lydia. "I was just saying to your friend, Miss Thorne, that O'Bannon's great on getting confessions."

"Really?" said Lydia. "I wonder why."

"Well," said the sheriff, ignoring the note of doubt in her wonder, "most criminals want to confess. It's a lonely thing—to have a secret and the whole world against you. He plays on that. And between you and I, Miss Thorne, there's some of this so-called psychology in it. You see, I prepare the way for him—telling how he always does get a confession, and how a confession last time saved the defendant from the chair, and a lot of stuff like that, and then he comes along, and I guess there's a little hypnotism in it too. Did you ever notice his eyes?"

"I noticed that he has them," answered Lydia.

Miss Bennett said that she had noticed them at once, as soon as he came into the room. Perhaps it was remembrance of them that made her add, "He won't be too hard on the poor girl, will he?"

"No, ma'am, he won't be hard at all," said the sheriff. "He'll just talk with her ten or fifteen minutes, and then she'll want to tell him the truth. I couldn't say how it's done."

Lydia suddenly stamped her foot.

"She's a fool if she does!" she said, biting into her words.

So this young man went in for being a woman tamer, did he?—the mistress downstairs ordered to be civil and the maid upstairs ordered to confess. If she had time, she thought, it would amuse her to show him that things did not run so smoothly as that. She almost wished that Evans wouldn't confess. It would be worth losing her jewels to see his face when he came down to announce his failure.

Steps overhead, the door opened, a voice called, "Sheriff, get your men up here, will you?"

The sheriff's face lit up.

"Didn't I tell you?" he said. "He's done it!" He hurried out of the room.

When, a few minutes later, the district attorney came down he found Miss Bennett alone. He looked about quickly.

"Where's Miss Thorne?" he said.

Miss Bennett had not wanted Lydia to go—she had urged her not to. What difference did the Emmonses make in comparison with the jewels? But now she sprang to her defense.

"She was forced to go. She had a train to catch—a long-

35

standing engagement. She was so sorry. She left all sorts of messages." This was not, strictly speaking, true.

O'Bannon smiled slightly.

"She does not seem to take much interest in the recovery of her jewels," he said.

"She has every confidence in you," said Miss Bennett flatteringly.

Miss Bennett herself had. Never, she thought, had she seen a man who inspired her with a more comfortable sense of leadership. She saw he was not pleased at Lydia's sudden departure.

He was not. He was furious at her. His feelings about her had flickered up and down like a flame. The vision of her going over her house alone, her hair down her back and a revolver in her hand, alone—except for Morson tagging on behind—moved him with a sense of her courage; and not only her courage but her lack of self-consciousness about it. She had spoken as if anyone would have done the same. Her hardness toward the criminal had repelled him, and when he went upstairs to interview Evans a new sensation waited for him.

The robbery had not released Evans from her regular duties. She had just finished packing Lydia's things for the visit to the Emmonses, and the bedroom where she had been detained had the disheveled look of a room which had just been packed and dressed in. The bed had not been made, though its pink silk cover had been smoothed over it to allow for the folding of dresses on it. Lydia's slippers—pink mules with an edging of fur—were kicked off beside it. Long trails of tissue paper were on the floor. O'Bannon saw it all with an eye trained to observe. He saw the book of verses on the table beside her bed, the picture of the good-looking young man on her dressing table. He smelled in the air the perfume of violets, a scent which his sense remembered as having lingered in her hair. All this he took in almost before he saw the pale, black-clad criminal standing vacantly in the midst of the disorder.

"Sit down," he said.

He spoke neither kindly nor commandingly, but as if to speak were the same thing as to accomplish. Evans sat down.

It was a curious picture of Lydia that emerged from the story she finally told him—a figure kind and generous and careless and cruel, and, it seemed to him above everything else, stupid, blind about life, the lives of those about her.

Evans had a lover, a young English footman who had served a term for stealing and just lately got out with an advanced case of tuberculosis. Evans, who had remained adamant to temptation when everything was going well with him, fell at the sight of his ill health. She had attempted, lonely and inefficient as she was, to do the trick by herself. It was Lydia's irritation over Evans' regret at the loss of the bracelet that had apparently decided the girl.

"If she was so glad to be relieved of the things I thought I'd help her a bit," she said bitterly.

What seemed to O'Bannon so incomprehensible was that Lydia shouldn't have known that the girl was in some sort of trouble. The sight of the room made him vividly aware of the intimacy of daily detail that any maid has in regard to her mistress— two women, and one going through hell.

He said to Miss Bennett after they had gone downstairs again: "Didn't Miss Thorne suspect that something was going wrong with the girl?"

Miss Bennett liked the district attorney so much that she felt a strong temptation, under the mask of discussing the case, to pour out to him all her troubles—the inevitable troubles of those whose lives were bound up with Lydia's. But her standards of good manners were too rigorous to allow her to yield.

"No, I'm afraid we didn't guess," she answered. "But now that we do know, is there anything we can do for the poor thing?"

"Not just now," he answered. "The case is clear against her. But when it comes to sentencing her you could do something. Anything Miss Thorne said in her favor would be taken into consideration by the judge."

"Tell me just what it is you want her to say," answered Miss Bennett, eager to help.

"It isn't what I want," O'Bannon replied with some irritation. "My duty is to present the case against her for the state. I'm telling what Miss Thorne can do if she feels that there are extenuating circumstances; if, for instance, she thinks that she herself has been careless about her valuables."

"She will, I'm sure," said Miss Bennett with more conviction than she felt, "because, between you and me, Mr. O'Bannon, she is careless. She lost a beautiful little bracelet the other—but when you're as young and lovely and rich as she is—"

She was interrupted by the district attorney's rather curt good-by.

"Do you want to drive back with me, sheriff?"

The sheriff did, and jumping in he murmured as they drove down the road: "She is all that. She's easy to look at all right. She's handsome, and yet not—not what I should call womanly. Look out at the turn. There's a hole as you get into the main road."

"Yes, I know about it," said O'Bannon.

37

CHAPTER V

When Lydia came back from the Emmonses late Monday afternoon she brought Bobby Dorset with her. Miss Bennett, who was arranging Morson's vases of flowers according to her more fastidious ideas, heard them come in, as noisy and high-spirited, she thought, as a couple of puppies. Lydia was so busy giving orders to have Bobby's room got ready and to have Eleanor telephoned to come over to dinner in case they wanted to play bridge, and sending the car for her, because Eleanor was so near-sighted she couldn't drive herself, and always let her chauffeur go home, and he had no telephone—so incompetent of Eleanor—that Miss Bennett had no chance to exchange a word with her. Besides, the poor lady was taken up with the horror of the approaching bridge game. She liked a mild rubber now and then, but not with Lydia, who scolded her after each hand, remembering every play.

Lydia, who was almost without physical or moral timidity, was always fighting against a subconscious horror, a repulsion rather than a fear, that life was just a futile, gigantic, patternless confusion, a tale told by an idiot, signifying nothing, which is the horror of all materialists. When she walked into her bedroom and found her things laid out just as usual, and a new maid—a Frenchwoman, brown and middle-aged and competent—waiting for her, just as Evans had waited, one of her moods of deep depression engulfed her, just as those who fear death are sometimes brought to a realization of its approach by some everyday symbol. Lydia did not fear death, but sometimes she hated life. She never asked if it were her own relation to life that was unsatisfactory.

When she came downstairs in a tea gown of orange and brown chiffon no one but Bobby noticed that her high spirits had all evaporated.

At table, before Morson and the footman, no one mentioned the subject of the robbery, but when they were back in the drawing-room Miss Bennett introduced it by asking: "Did the new woman hook you up right? Will she do, dear?"

Lydia shrugged her shoulders, not stopping to think that Miss Bennett had spent one whole day in intelligence offices and a morning on the telephone in her effort to replace Evans.

The older woman was silenced by the shrug—not hurt, but disappointed—and in the silence Bobby said: "Oh, what happened about Evans? They took her away?"

Lydia answered, with a contemptuous raising of her chin, "She confessed—she always was a goose."

38

"That didn't prove it," returned Miss Bennett with spirit. "It was the wisest thing to do. The district attorney—my dear girls, if I were your age, and that man—"

"Look out!" said Lydia. "He's a great friend of Eleanor's."

"Of Eleanor?" exclaimed Miss Bennett. She was not and never had been a vain woman, but she was always astonished at men caring for a type of femininity different from her own. She liked Eleanor, but she thought her dry and unattractive, and she didn't see what a brilliant, handsome creature like O'Bannon could see in her. "Is he, really?"

"Yes, he is," said Eleanor coolly. Experience had taught her an excellent manner in this situation.

"I wish you had waited, Lydia," Miss Bennett went on. "It was very impressive the way he managed Evans, almost like a hypnotic influence. She told him everything. She seemed to give herself over into his hands. It was almost like a miracle. A moment before she had been so hostile—a miracle taking place right there in Lydia's bedroom."

Lydia, who had been bending over reorganizing the fire, suddenly straightened up with the poker in her hand and said quickly, "Where? Taking place where?"

"In your room, dear. Evans was shut up there."

"That man in my room!" said Lydia, and her whole face seemed to blaze with anger.

"It never occurred to me that you would object, my dear. He said he—"

"It should have occurred to you. I hate the idea—that drunken attorney in my bedroom. It's not decent!"

"Lydia!" said Miss Bennett.

Eleanor spoke in a voice as cold as steel.

"What do you mean by calling Mr. O'Bannon a drunken attorney?"

"He drinks—Bobby says so."

"I did not say so!"

"Why, Bobby, you did!"

"I said he used to drink when he was in college."

"Oh, well, a reformed drunkard," said Lydia, shrugging her shoulders. "I can't imagine your doing such a thing, Benny, except that you always do anything that anyone asks you to do."

Her tone was more insulting than her words, and Miss Bennett did the most sensible thing she could think of—she got up and left the room. Lydia stood on the hearthrug, tapping her foot, breathing quickly, her jaw set.

"I think Bennett's losing her mind," she said.

39

"I think you are," said Eleanor. "What possible difference does it make?"

"You say that because you're crazy about this man. Perhaps if I were in love with him I'd lose all my sense of delicacy too; but as it is—"

Eleanor got up.

"I think I'll take my lack of delicacy home," she said. "Tell Morson to send for the motor, will you, Bobby? Good night Lydia. I've had a perfectly horrid evening."

"Good night," said Lydia with a fierce little beck of her head.

Bobby saw Eleanor to the car, and sat with her some time in the hall while it was being brought round.

"No one could blame you for being furious; but you're not angry at her, are you, Eleanor?" he said.

"Of course I'm angry!" answered Eleanor. "She's too impossible, Bobby. You can't keep on with people who let you in for this sort of thing. I could have had a perfectly pleasant evening at home—and to come out for a row like this!"

"She doesn't do it often."

"Often! No, there wouldn't be any question then."

"She's been perfectly charming at the Emmonses'—gay and friendly, and everyone crazy about her. And by the way, Eleanor, I didn't say O'Bannon was a drunkard."

"Of course you didn't," said Eleanor.

"But he used to go on the most smashing sprees in college, and I told her about one of those and made her promise not to tell."

"A lot that would influence Lydia."

The car was at the door now, and as he put her into it he asked, "Oh, don't you feel so sorry for her sometimes that you could almost weep over her?"

"I certainly do not!" said Eleanor.

Turning from the front door, Bobby ran upstairs and knocked at Miss Bennett's door. He found her sunk in an enormous chair, looking very pathetic and more like an unhappy child than a middle-aged woman.

"It isn't bearable," she said. "Life under these conditions is too disagreeable. I don't complain of her never noticing all the little sacrifices one makes—all the trouble one takes for her sake. But when she's absolutely rude—just vulgarly, grossly rude as she was this evening—"

"Miss Bennett," said Bobby seriously, "when things go wrong with women they cry, and when things go wrong with men they swear. Lydia takes a little from both sexes. These outbursts are her equivalent for feminine tears or masculine profanity."

40

Miss Bennett looked up at him with her starlike eyes shining with emotion.

"But someone must teach her that she can't behave like that. I can't do it. I can only teach by being kind—endlessly kind—and she can't learn from that. So the best thing for both of us is for me to leave her and let someone else try."

Bobby sat down and took her thin aristocratic hand in both of his.

"No one can teach her, dear Benny," he said. "But life can—and will. That's my particular nightmare—that people like Lydia get broken by life—and it's always such a smash. That's why I'm content to stand by without, as most of my friends think, due regard for my own self-respect. That's why I do hope you'll contrive to. That's why she seems to me the most pathetic person I know. She almost makes me cry."

"Pathetic!" said Miss Bennett with something approaching a snort.

"Yes, like a child playing with a dynamite fuse. Even to-night she seemed to me pathetic. She can't afford to alienate the few people who really care for her—you and Eleanor and—well, of course, she won't alienate me, whatever she does."

"But she takes advantage of our affection," said Miss Bennett.

Bobby stood up.

"You bet she does!" he said. "She'll have something bitter waiting for me now when I go down, something she'll have forgotten by to-morrow and I'll remember as long as I live."

He smiled perfectly gayly and left the room. He found Lydia strolling about the drawing-room, softly whistling to herself.

"Well," she said, "my party seems to have broken up early."

"Broken's the word," answered Bobby.

"Isn't Eleanor absurd?" said Lydia. "She loves so to be superior—'Order my carriage'—like the virtuous duchess in a melodrama."

"She doesn't seem absurd to me," said Bobby.

"Oh, you've been tiptoeing about binding up everybody's wounds, I suppose," she answered. "Did you tell them that you knew I didn't mean a word I said? Ah, yes, I see you did. Well, I did mean every single word, and more. Upon my word, I wish you'd mind your own business, Bobby."

"I will," said Bobby, and got up and left the room.

He went out and walked quickly up and down the flat stones under the grape arbor. The moon was not up, and the stars twinkled fiercely in the crisp cool air. He thought of other women—lovelier and kinder than Lydia. What kept him in this bondage to her? All the time he was asking the question he was aware of her image in her orange tea gown against the dark woodwork of the room, and suddenly, before he knew it—certainly before he had made any resolve to return—he was back in the doorway, saying,

"Would you like to play a game of piquet?"

She nodded, and they sat down at the card table. Bobby's faint resentment had gone in ten minutes, but it was longer before Lydia, laying down her cards, said, as if they had just been talking about her misdeeds instead of merely thinking about them, "But Benny is awfully obstinate, isn't she? I mean the way she goes on doing things the way she thinks I ought to like them instead of finding out the way I do like."

"She's very sweet—Benny is."

"And that's just what makes everyone think me so terrible— the contrast. She's sweet, but she wants her own way just the same. Whereas I—"

"You don't want your own way, Lydia?"

They nearly fought it out all over again. This time it was Lydia who stopped the discussion with a sudden change of manner.

"The truth is, Bobby," she said with an unexpected gentleness, "that I feel dreadfully about Evans. You don't know how fond you get of a person who's about you all the time like that."

"Horrid that they'll rob you, isn't it?"

"Yes." Lydia stared thoughtfully before her. "I think what I mind most is that she wouldn't tell me—kept denying it, as if I were her enemy—and then in the first second she confessed to the district attorney."

"Oh, well, that's his profession."

She seemed to think profoundly, and her next sentence surprised him.

"Do you think there's anything really between him and Eleanor? I couldn't bear to have Eleanor marry a man like that."

Bobby, trying to be tactful, answered that he was sure Eleanor wouldn't, but as often happens to consciously tactful people, he failed to please.

"Oh," said Lydia, "you mean that you think he's crazy about her?"

"Mercy, no!" said Bobby. "I shouldn't think Eleanor was his type at all, except perhaps as a friend. It's the chorus-girl type that really stirs him."

"Oh, is it?" said Lydia, and took up the cards again.

They played two hours, and the game calmed her but could not save her from the blackness of her mood. It came upon her, as it always did if it were coming, a few minutes after she had got into bed, turned out her light and had begun to discover that sleep was not close at hand. Life seemed to her all effort without purpose. She felt like a martyr at the stake; only she had no vision to bear her company. She felt her loneliness to be not the result of anything she said or did, but inevitable. There seemed to be nothing in the universe but chaos and herself.

She turned on her light again and read until almost morning. Nights like this were not unusual with Lydia.

CHAPTER VI

Joe Thorne had been fond of telling a story about Lydia in her childhood—in the days before Miss Bennett came to them. After some tremendous scene of naughtiness and punishment, she had come to him and said: "Father, if you're not angry at me any more, I'm not angry at you." It was characteristic of her still. She was not afraid to come forward and make up, but she was shy with the spoken word. She couldn't make an emotional apology, but she managed to convey in all sorts of dumb ways that she wanted to be friends—she contrived to remember some long ungratified wish of Benny's, whether it were a present, or a politeness to some old friend, or sometimes only an errand that Benny had never been able to get her to do. There was always a definite symbol that Lydia was sorry, and she was always forgiven.

Part of Eleanor's sense of her own superiority to the world lay in being more than usually impervious to emotion. Besides she had expressed herself satisfactorily at the time by leaving the house, so that she forgave too. Only of course a scene like that is never without consequences—everybody's endurance had snapped a few more strands like a fraying rope. And there were consequences, too, in Lydia's own nature. She seemed to have become permanently wrong-headed and violent on any subject even remotely connected with the district attorney.

This was evident a few days later when a voice proclaiming itself that of Judge Homans' secretary asked her if she could make it convenient to stop at the judge's chambers that afternoon to give the court some information in regard to a former maid of hers—Evans. Lydia's tone showed that it was not at all convenient. It seemed at one instant as if she were about to refuse point-blank to go. Then she yielded, and from that minute it became clear that her mind was continually occupied with the prospect of the visit.

Late in the afternoon she appeared before the judge's desk in his little room, lined with shelves of calf-bound volumes. It was a chilly November afternoon, and she had just come from tea at the golf club after eighteen holes. She was wrapped in a bright golden-brown coat, and a tomato-colored hat was pulled down over her brows.

The judge, for no reason ascertainable, had imagined Miss Thorne, the landed proprietor, the owner of jewels of value, as a dignified woman of thirty. He looked up in surprise over his spectacles. His first idea—he lived much out of the world—was that a mistake had been made and that an unruly female offender had been brought to him, not a complaining witness.

Even after this initial misunderstanding was explained the interview did not go well. The judge was a man of sixty, clean shaven and of a waxy hue. From his high, narrow brow all his lines flowed outward. His chin was heavy and deeply creased, and he had a way at times of drawing it in to meet his heavy, hunched shoulders. A natural interest in the continuity of his own thought, joined to fifteen years of pronouncements from the bench, rendered him impervious to interruption. He now insisted on reviewing the case of Evans, while Lydia sat tossing back first one side and then the other of her heavy coat and thinking—almost saying, "Oh, the tiresome old man! Why does he tell me all this? Doesn't he know that it was my jewels that were stolen?" She began to tap her foot, a sound which to those who knew Lydia well was regarded almost as the rattle of the rattlesnake. The judge began to draw his monologue to a close.

"The district attorney tells me that you feel that there was some carelessness on your own part which might be considered in a measure as constituting an extenuating circumstance—"

He got no further.

"The district attorney says so?" said Lydia, and if he had quoted the authority of the janitor's boy her tone could not have expressed more contemptuous surprise.

His Honor, however, missed it.

"Yes," he went on, "Mr. O'Bannon tells me that the charge of your safe, without supervision—"

"Mr. O'Bannon is completely misinformed," said Lydia, shutting her eyes and raising her eyebrows.

The judge turned his head squarely to look at her.

"You mean," he said, "that you do not feel that there was any contributory carelessness which might in part explain, without in any true sense excusing—"

"Certainly not," said Lydia. "And I have never said anything to anyone that would make them think so."

"I have been misinformed as to your attitude," said the judge.

"Evidently," said Lydia, and almost at once brought the interview to a close by leaving the room.

As she walked down the path to her car a figure came out of the shadow as if it had been waiting for her. It was the same traffic policeman who had stopped her on her way to Eleanor's. He took off his brown cap. She saw his round, pugnacious head and the uncertain curve of his mouth. He was a nice-looking man, and younger than she had supposed—quite boyish in fact. She caught a

45

glimpse of some sort of ribbon on his breast—the croix de guerre. She looked straight at him with interest, and saw that he was tense with embarrassment.

"I believe I have something of yours," he said. "I want to give it back." He was fumbling in his pocket. She couldn't really permit that.

"Bribed people," she thought, "must be content to remain bribed." She walked rapidly toward her car without answering. The chauffeur opened the door for her.

"Home," she said, and drove away.

An hour or so later the judge was giving a description of the interview to the district attorney. It began as a general indictment of the irresponsibility of the wealthy young people of to-day, touching on their dress, appearance and manners. Then it descended suddenly to the particular case.

"She came into this room in a hat the color of a flamingo"—the judge's color sense was not good—"and her skirts almost to her knees; as bold—well, I wouldn't like to tell you what my first idea was on seeing her. She was as hard as—I could have told her that some of her own father's methods were not strictly legal, only the courts were more lenient in those days. A ruthless fellow—Joe Thorne. Do you know this girl?"

"I've met her," said O'Bannon.

"She made a very unfavorable impression on me," said Judge Homans. "I don't know when a young woman of agreeable appearance—she has considerable beauty—has made such an unfavorable impression." And His Honor added, as if the two remarks had nothing to do with each other, "I shall give this unfortunate maid a very light sentence."

The district attorney bowed. It was exactly what he had always intended.

But a sentence which sounded light to Judge Homans—not less than three and a half nor more than fifteen years—sounded heavy to Lydia. She was horrified. The recent visit which, under Mrs. Galton's auspices, she had paid to a man's prison was in her mind—the darkness, the crowded cells, the pale abnormal-looking prisoners, the smell, the guards, the silence. She simply would not allow Evans to spend fifteen years in such torture. She was all the more determined because she knew, without once admitting it, that she might have prevented it.

She read the sentence in the local newspaper at breakfast— she breakfasted in bed—and the next minute she was up and in Miss Bennett's room.

"This is a little too much," she said, walking in so fast that her

46

silk dressing gown stood out like a rose-colored balloon. "Fifteen years! Those men must be mad! Come, Benny, put on your things. You must go with me to the district attorney's office and have this arranged. Imagine it! After her confessing too! I said she was wrong to confess."

But when she reached the office she found no one there but Miss Finnegan, the stenographer.

"Where's Mr. O'Bannon?" she asked as if she had an engagement with him which he had broken.

Miss Finnegan raised her head from her keys and looked at the unexpected visitor in a tomato-colored hat, whose feet had sounded so sharp and quick on the stairs and who had thrown open the door so violently.

"Mr. O'Bannon's in court," she answered in a tone which seemed to suggest that almost anyone would know that. By this time, mounting the stairs with more dignity, Miss Bennett entered, appealing and conciliatory.

"We want so much to see him," she murmured.

Miss Finnegan softened and said that she'd telephone over to the courthouse. He might be able to get over for a minute. She telephoned and hung up the receiver in silence.

"When will he be here?" demanded Lydia.

"When he's at liberty," Miss Finnegan answered coldly.

Waiting did not calm Lydia nor the atmosphere of the office, which proclaimed O'Bannon's power. People kept coming in with the same question—when could they see the district attorney? An old foreigner was there who kept muttering something to Miss Finnegan in broken English.

"Yes, but then your son ought to plead," Miss Finnegan kept saying over and over again, punctuating her sentence with quick roulades on the typewriter.

There was a thin young man with shifty eyes, and a local lawyer with a strong flavor of the soil about him.

Miss Bennett watched Lydia anxiously. The girl was not accustomed to being kept waiting. Her bank, her dentist, the shops where she dealt had long ago learned that it saved everybody trouble to serve Miss Thorne first.

At last O'Bannon entered. Lydia sprang up.

"Mr. O'Bannon—" she began. He held up his hand.

"One minute," he said.

He was listening to the story of the old woman, not even glancing in Lydia's direction; yet something in the bend of his head, in the strain of his effort to keep his eyes on his interlocutor and his mind on what was being told him made Miss Bennett believe he was acutely aware of their presence. Yet Lydia patiently bore even this delay. Miss Bennett drew a breath of relief. The girl had evidently come resolved to show her better side. The impression was strengthened when he approached them. Lydia's manner was gentle and dignified.

"Mr. O'Bannon," said she, "I feel distressed at the sentence of my maid—Evans."

Miss Bennett looked on like a person seeing a vision—Lydia had never seemed—had never been like this—gentle, feminine, well, there was no other word for it, sweet—poignantly sweet. She did not see how anyone could resist her, and glancing at the district attorney she saw he was not resisting, on the contrary, with bent head, and his queer light eyes fixed softly on Lydia's he was drinking in every tone of her voice. Their voices sank lower and lower until they were almost whispering to each other, so low that Miss Bennett thought fantastically that anybody coming in unexpectedly might have thought they were lovers.

"She isn't a criminal," Lydia was saying. "She was tempted, and she has confessed. Won't you help me to save her?"

"I can't," he whispered back. "It's too late. She's been sentenced."

"Too late, perhaps, by the regular methods—but there are always others. You have so much power—you give people the feeling you can do anything." He shook his head, still gazing at her. "You give me that feeling. Do this for me."

"You could have done it yourself, so easily, before she was sentenced."

"I know, I know. That's why I care so. Oh, Mr. O'Bannon, just for a moment, you and I—" Her voice sank so that Miss Bennett could not hear what she said, but she saw her put her hand on his arm like a person taking possession of her own belongings. Then there was no use in listening any more, for a complete silence had fallen between them; they did not even seem to be breathing.

The district attorney suddenly raised his head with a quick shake, like a dog coming out of water, and stepped back.

"It can't be done," he said. "If I were willing to break the law into pieces, I can't do it."

Lydia's brow darkened. "You mean you won't," she said.

"No," he answered quietly. "I mean just what I say. I can't. Remember you have had two chances to help the girl—at the first complaint, and in your conversation with the judge. Why didn't you do it then?"

Why hadn't she? She didn't know, but she answered hastily:

"I did not understand—"

"You wouldn't understand," he returned, in that quiet, terrible tone that made her think somehow of Ilseboro. "I tried to tell you and you wouldn't wait to hear, and the judge tried to tell you and you wouldn't listen. People don't often get three chances in this world, Miss Thorne."

His tone maddened her, in combination with her own failure. "Are you taking it upon yourself to reprove me, Mr. O'Bannon?" she asked.

"I'm taking it upon myself to tell you how things are," he answered.

"I don't believe it is the way they are," she said.

Angry as she was, she did not mean the phrase to sound as insulting as it did. She meant that there must be some unsuspected avenue of approach; but her quick tone and insolent manner made the words themselves sound like the final insult.

O'Bannon simply turned from her, and holding up his hand to the shifty-eyed boy said clearly, "I'll see you now, Gray."

There was nothing for Lydia to do but accept her dismissal. She flounced out of the room, and all the way home in the car shocked Miss Bennett by her epithets. "Insolent country lout" was the mildest of them.

A few days afterward Miss Thorne moved back to New York to the house in the East Seventies. Miss Bennett, who hated the country, partly because there she was more under Lydia's thumb, rejoiced at being back in New York. She had many friends—was much more personally popular than her charge—and in town she could see them more easily. Every morning after she had finished her housekeeping she went out and walked round the reservoir. She liked to walk, planting her little feet as precisely as if she were dancing or skating. Then there was usually some necessary shopping for Lydia or the house or herself; then luncheon, and afterward for an hour or two her own work. She was a member of endless committees, entertainments for charitable purposes, hospital boards, reform associations. Then before five she was at home, behind the tea table, waiting on Lydia, engaged in getting rid of people whom Lydia didn't want to see and keeping those whom Lydia would want to see but had forgotten. And then dinner—at home if Lydia was giving a party; but most often both women dined out.

The winter was notable for Lydia's sudden friendship or flirtation, or affair as it was variously described, with Stephen Albee, the ex-governor of a great state. It would have seemed more natural if he had been one of Eleanor's discoveries, but he was not—he was Lydia's own find. Eleanor, with all her airs of a young old maid, had

49

never been known to distinguish any man lacking in the physical attractions of youth. Albee, though he had been a fine-looking man once and still had a certain magnificent leonine appearance, was over fifty and showed his years. He had come to New York to conduct an important Federal investigation, and the masterly manner in which he was doing it led to presidential prophecies. Lydia's friends were beginning to murmur that it would be just like Lydia to end in the White House. Besides, the governor was rich, the owner of silver mines and a widower. It was noticed that Lydia was more respectful to him than she had ever been to anyone, followed his lead intellectually, and quoted him to the verge of being comic.

"It is painful to me," Eleanor said, "to watch the process of Lydia's discovering politics. Last Monday the existence of the Federal constitution dawned upon her, and next week states' rights may emerge."

It was equally painful to the governor's old friends to watch the even less graceful process of his discovery of social life. The two friends adventured mutually. If Lydia sat all day listening to his investigation, he appeared hardly less regularly in her opera box.

Oddly enough, they had met at a prison-reform luncheon given by the same noble women whose presence at her house had so much irritated Lydia. The object of the luncheon was to advertise the cause, to inspire workers, to raise money. Albee was the principal speaker, not because he had any special interest in prison reform, but because he was the most conspicuous public figure in New York at the moment, and as he was known not to be an orator, everyone was eager to hear him speak. Mrs. Galton, the chairman of the meeting, was shocked by his reactionary views on prisons when he expounded them to her in an attempt to evade her invitation; but with the sound worldliness which every reformer must acquire she knew that his name was far more important to her cause than his views, and with a little judicious flattery she roped him into promising he would come and say a few words—not, he specially insisted, a speech. Mrs. Galton agreed, knowing that no speaker in the world, certainly no masculine speaker, could resist the appeal of a large, warm, admiring audience when once he got to his feet. "The only difficulty will be stopping him," she thought rather sadly. It would be wise, too, she thought, to put someone next to him at luncheon who would please him. Flattery from an ugly old woman like herself wouldn't be enough. Then she remembered Lydia, whom, after their unfortunate meeting at luncheon in the autumn, she had taken through one of the men's prisons in an effort to enlist the girl's coöperation. They had had conferences over Evans too, for Lydia had not remained utterly indifferent to Evans' situation, had indeed permitted, even urged, Miss Bennett to go to visit the girl and see what could be done for her.

Miss Thorne accepted the invitation to attend the luncheon; and then, as cold-bloodedly as a diplomat might make use of a lovely courtesan, Mrs. Galton put her next to the great man at the speakers' table, where of course so young, idle and useless a person had no right to be.

The governor arrived very late, with his fingers in his waistcoat pocket to indicate to all who saw him hurrying in between the crowded tables that he had been unavoidably detained and had spent the last half hour in agonized contemplation of his watch. As a matter of fact, he had been reading the papers at his club, wishing to cut down the hour of too much food and too much noise which he knew would precede the hour of too much speaking. He knew he would sit next to Mrs. Galton, whom he esteemed as a wise and good philanthropist but dreaded as a companion.

Everything began as he feared. He took his place on Mrs. Galton's right, with an apology for having been detained— unavoidably. It had looked at one time as if he could not get there, but of course his feeling for the great work—

Mrs. Galton, who had been through all this hundreds of times and knew he had never intended to arrive a minute earlier than he did, smiled warmly, and said how fortunate they counted themselves in having obtained an hour of the time of a man whom all the world—

On the contrary, the governor esteemed it a privilege to speak on behalf of a cause which commanded the sympathy—

It was a turning point, indeed, in the history of any cause, when a man like the governor—

They would have gone on like this through luncheon, but at this moment a sudden rustling at his side made the governor turn, and there—later a good deal than he had contrived to be—was Lydia, Lydia in a tight plain dress and a small plumed hat that made her look like a crested serpent. Mrs. Galton introduced them, and with a sigh of relief settled back to eating her lunch and running over her own introductory remarks in the comfortable certainty that the governor would give her no more trouble.

He didn't. He looked at Lydia, and all his heavy politeness dropped from him. His eyes twinkled, and he said, "Come, my dear young lady, let us save time by your telling me who you are and what you do and why you are here."

This amused Lydia.

"I think," she said, "that that is the best conversational

51

opening I ever heard. Well, I suppose I ought to say that I am here to listen to you."

"Yes, yes—perhaps," answered Albee, with a somewhat political wave of his hand, "in the same sense in which I came here to meet you—because fate, luck, divine interposition arranged it so. But why, according to your own limited views, are you here?"

"Oh, in response to a noble impulse. Don't you ever have them?"

"I did—I did when I was your age," said the governor, and he leaned back and studied her with open admiration, which somehow in a man of his reputation was not offensive.

"Why are you here yourself?" said Lydia, giving him a gentle look to convey that she was very grateful to him for thinking her so handsome.

"Why, I just told you," answered the governor, "because Fate said to herself: 'Now here's poor old Stephen Albee's been having a dull hard time of it. Let's have something pleasant happen to him. Let's have him meet Miss Thorne.'"

A lady on Lydia's other side, who gave her life to the reform of criminals and particularly hated those who remained outside of penal institutions, was horrified by what she considered the flirtatious tone of the conversation. She could hear—in fact she listened—that several meetings had been arranged before the governor's time came to speak.

Everything worked out exactly as Mrs. Galton had intended. The governor—who had expected to say that he was heart and soul with this great cause, to rehearse a few historic examples of prison mismanagement, to confide to his audience that a man of national reputation was at that moment waiting to see him about something of international importance, and then to get away in time to play a few holes of golf before dark—rose to his feet, fired with the determination to make a good speech, good enough to impress Lydia; and he did. He had a simple direct manner of speaking, so that no one noticed that his sentences themselves were rather oratorical and emotional. Most speakers, too many at least, have just the opposite technic—an oratorical manner and no matter behind it. He gave the impression, without actually saying so, that the only reason he had not given his life to prison reform was that the larger duty of the public service called him, and the only reason why he did not swamp his audience with the technical details of the subject was that it was too painful, too shocking.

There was great and sincere applause as he sat down. Workers were inspired, subscriptions did flow in. Before the next speaker rose, Lydia, in sight of the whole room, walked out, followed by the great man, who had explained hastily to Mrs. Galton that he was already late for an engagement with a man of national reputation who was waiting to discuss a matter of international importance. Mrs. Galton nodded amiably. She had little further use for the governor.

The next day Lydia went downtown to hear him conducting his investigation, and was impressed by the spectacle of his dominating will and crystalline mind in action. She came every day. Her life heretofore had not stimulated her to intellectual endeavor, but now she discovered that she had a good, keen mind. She learned the procedure of the investigation, remembered the evidence, read books—Wellman on Cross-Examination and the Adventures of Sergeant Ballentine. She enjoyed herself immensely. It was the best game she had ever played. The vision of a vicarious career as the wife of a great politician was now always in the back of her mind.

Eleanor, with her superior intellectual equipment, might laugh at Lydia's late discovery of the political field; but Lydia's knowledge was not theoretical and remote, like Eleanor's. It was alive, vivified by her energy and coined into the daily action of her life. With half Eleanor's brains she was twice as effective.

She admired Albee deeply, almost dangerously, and she wanted to admire him more. She enjoyed all the symbols of his power. She liked the older, more important men of her acquaintance to come suing to her for an opportunity of meeting Albee socially. She liked to watch other women trying to draw him away from her. She even liked the way the traffic policemen would let her car through when he was in it. She liked all these things, not from vanity, as many girls would have liked them, but because they constantly held before her eyes the picture of Albee as a superman. And if Albee were a superman the problem of her life was solved. Then everything would be simple—to give her youth and beauty and money, her courage and knowledge of the world to making him supreme. It was true that he had not as yet asked her to marry him—had not even made love to her, unless admiration is love-making—but to Lydia that was a secondary consideration. The first thing was to make up her own mind.

She had two great problems to face. At first he did not want to go out at all—did not want to enter her field. He appeared to think, as so many Americans do, that there was something trivial, almost immoral, in meeting your fellow creatures except in professional relations. The second problem was worse, that having overcome his reluctance, he began to like it too much, to take it too seriously. He had never had time for it before, he said, but actually he must have felt excluded from it, either at college, or as a young man in the legislature of his state.

The first time he went to the opera with her—he was genuinely fond of music—she noticed this. Lydia's box was next to Mrs. Little's. The newspapers made her name impressive, but her slim white-haired presence made her more so. Lydia herself admired her, and if ever she thought of her own old age she thought she would like to be like Mrs. Little—a wish very unlikely of realization, for Mrs. Little had been molded by traditional obligations and sacrifices to duties which Lydia had never acknowledged.

As they were waiting in the crowded lobby of the Thirty-ninth Street entrance—all the faces above velvets and furs peering out and all the footmen's faces peering in and everyone chattering and shouting and so little apparently accomplished in the way of clearing the crowd—Albee said: "Mrs. Little has asked me to dine on the sixteenth."

Lydia caught something complaisant in the tone. The idea that he could be flattered by such an invitation was distasteful to her.

"Did you accept?" she asked in a cold tone that she tried to make noncommittal.

Fortunately politics had taught Albee caution. He had not accepted. He had said that he would let the great lady know in the morning.

"Do you think that sort of thing will amuse you?"

He answered that it would amuse him if she were going, and against her better judgment she allowed herself to believe that the eagerness in his voice had been occasioned by the promised opportunity of seeing her.

The fancy ball was more serious. The Pulsifers were giving it in their great ballroom just before Lent. Lydia and Miss Bennett were discussing costumes one afternoon at tea time when Albee was announced. Lydia had been at his investigation that morning, and had never admired him more.

"It's the Pulsifers we're talking about," said Miss Bennett as he entered. "Lydia wants to be a Japanese, but there'll be lots of them. I want her to go as an American Indian."

With a vivid recollection of him deciding a struggle that morning between two lawyers, Lydia felt ashamed, humbled, that she should be presented to him as occupied with such a subject as a fancy costume. His voice cut in.

"Oh, yes, the Pulsifers! I had a card this morning." It was the same complaisant tone—as if it mattered whether he had or not.

"Oh, do go!" cried Miss Bennett. She meant to be helpful, and added the first thing that came into her head. "You would make a wonderful Roman senator. I'll arrange your costume for you."

In a flash Lydia saw him before her, bare legged, bare armed, bare throated. She recoiled, though of course it was not his fault. If Benny had said a doge or a cardinal; but glancing at her friend she saw he was not suited to either rôle. He was not fine and thin and subtle. He was the type of a Roman senator.

"It would be a great temptation to go—to see Miss Thorne as an Indian," he answered, smiling his admiration at her.

"I don't think I shall go," said Lydia, waving her head slightly. "I don't think it's dignified—dressing up like monkeys."

Miss Bennett looked up surprised. Lydia had been so interested in the whole subject a few minutes before. She thought the girl was growing uncommonly capricious. Albee caught the note at once.

"If they would let me go as a spectator—" he began.

"That spoils it, you know," Miss Bennett answered, but Lydia interrupted:

"Of course, they'd be glad to get the governor on any terms."

But the question was more simply settled. Albee was summoned to Washington to testify before a committee of the Senate which under the guise of helping him was actually trying to steal the political thunder of his investigation and Lydia, with her Indian costume just completed—and Benny's, too, from a Longhi picture—abandoned the whole thing and went off to Washington to hear the great man testify carrying the reluctant Miss Bennett with her.

Bobby Dorset, who had said immediately just what Lydia had longed to hear Albee say—that parties like that were more trouble than they were worth—had been coerced by Lydia into going. She had made him get a Greek warrior's costume, in which he was very splendid. He was left with his costume and his party, and no Lydia to make it pleasant.

He had come in late one afternoon and had stayed on, as he often did to dinner. In the middle of the meal Lydia was called away—Governor Albee wanted to speak to her on the telephone. She sprang up from the table and left the room. Miss Bennett looked pathetically at Bobby.

"It's to decide whether we go to Washington to-morrow," she said.

"To Washington?"

"The governor is going to testify before a Senate committee

55

and has invited us to come. It will be very interesting," Miss Bennett added loyally.

"But the Pulsifers?"

"Oh, I'm surprised Lydia cares so little for that. Of course, at my age, I'm grateful to escape it."

"Oh, Benny," said Bobby, "you're not a bit! You'd much rather go to it than to any old Senate committee. You love parties for the same reason that the lamb loved Mary."

"You make me seem very frivolous—at fifty-five," said Miss Bennett.

Then Lydia came back from the pantry, her eyes bright, and laid her hand on her companion's shoulder, a rare caress, as she passed.

"We're going, Benny. It isn't closed to the public." Her whole face was softened and lit by her pleasure.

Bobby thought, "Can it be she really cares for that old war horse?"

56

CHAPTER VII

It was great fun traveling with Albee. He had engaged a drawing-room on the Congressional Limited, and with a forethought, old-fashioned but agreeable, had provided newspapers and magazines and a box of candy. His secretary was hovering near with letters to be signed. The conductor came and asked whether everything was all right, governor, and people passed the door deliberately, staring in to get a glimpse of the great man; and Lydia could see that they were murmuring, "That's Albee, you know, he's going down to testify."

Lydia did not know Washington at all. She had been taken there once as a child by one of the energetic young American governesses—had gone to Mt. Vernon by boat and home by trolley, had whispered in the rotunda and looked at the statues and seen the House and been secretly glad that the Senate was in secret session so that she couldn't see that, and there would be time to go up the monument—something that she really had enjoyed—not only on account of the view, but because her governess was afraid of elevators and was terrified in the slow, jerky ascent. Then during the period of her engagement to Ilseboro she had been at one or two dinners at the British embassy. But that had been long ago, before the days of her discovery of the Federal Constitution. Of governmental Washington she knew nothing.

The Senate committee met at ten the next morning. There was a good deal of interest in the hearing, and the corridors were full of people waiting for the doors to open. Miss Bennett and Lydia were taken in first through a private room to assure their having good seats. Lydia found the committee room beautiful—more like a gentleman's library than an office—wide, high windows looking out on the Capitol grounds, tall bookcases with glass doors and blue-silk curtains, a huge polished-wood table in the center; with chairs about it for the senators.

She recognized them as they came in from Albee's description—the neat blue-eyed senator who looked like a little white fox, his enemy; the fat blond young man, full of words and smiles, who was a most ineffective friend; and the large suave chairman, in a tightly fitting plum-colored suit, with a grace of manner that kept you from knowing whether he were friend or foe.

Not that you would have suspected from anyone's manner that there was such a thing as enmity in the world—they were all so quiet and friendly. Indeed, when Albee came in he was talking—

57

"chatting" would be a better word—with the little fox-faced senator against whom he had so specially warned Lydia. The whole tone was as if eight or ten hard-working men had called in a friend to help them out on the facts.

Lydia thought it very exciting, knowing as she did how much of hate and party politics lay behind the hearing. She was only dimly aware that her own future depended on the impression Albee might now make upon her. In his own investigation in New York he was the chief, but here he would be attacked, ruled against, tripped up if possible. There he was a general, here he was a duelist. She saw several senators glancing at her, asking who she was, and guessed that the answer was that she was the girl Albee was in love with, engaged to, making a fool of himself over—something like that. She didn't mind. She felt proud to be identified with him. She looked at him as he sat down at the chairman's right, and tried to think how she would feel if she were saying to herself, "There's my husband." Could you marry a man for whom you felt an immovable physical coldness? She thought of Dan O'Bannon's kiss, and the continuity of her thought broke up in a tangle of emotion—even there in the white morning light of that remote committee room.

The hearing was beginning; it was beginning with phrases like, "The committee would be glad, governor, if you would tell us in your own words—"

"If I might be permitted, Mister Senator, my understanding is—"

Again and again she saw the trap laid for him and thought with alarm that there was no escape, and then saw that with no effort, with just a turn of his easy wrist, he escaped, and what was more remarkable, had told the truth—yes, as she thought it over, it was nearly the truth. He was particularly successful with the fox-faced senator, whose only interest seemed to be to get the governor to say something that would look badly in newspaper headlines. She grasped Albee's method after a few instances. It was to make the senator define and redefine his question until whatever odium attached to the subject would fall on the questioner, not the answerer.

After fifteen minutes she knew that he was a match for them—his mind was quicker, subtler and more powerful. He made them all seem mentally clumsy and evilly disposed. He could put their questions, even the hostile ones, so much better than they could. Again and again, with a gentle, an almost loving smile, he would say, "I think, Mister Senator, if you will allow me, that what you really mean to ask in that last question is whether—" And a clear

58

exact statement of the confused ideas of the senator would follow, as the senator, with an abashed nod, would be forced to admit.

Lydia, unused to this sort of thing, thought it little short of a miracle that anyone's mind could work as well as that under such pressure. He seemed to her a superman.

After the hearing they lunched downstairs in the airless basement in which the Fathers of the Senate are provided with excellent Southern dishes, served by white-jacketed negroes. Lydia met most of the notables, even the fox-faced senator, who, she was told was very much of a ladies' man. She was for the first time a satellite, a part of the suite of a great man, and glad to be.

Then, after luncheon, Benny having tactfully expressed a wish to go back to the hotel and rest, as they were going out to dinner, Lydia and the governor took a walk along the banks of the Potomac. March is very springlike in Washington. The fruit trees were beginning to bud and the air was mild and still, so that the river reflected the monument like a looking-glass.

"You seemed to me very wonderful this morning," she said.

He turned to her.

"If I were thirty years younger you wouldn't say that to me with impunity."

"If you were thirty years younger you would seem like an inefficient boy compared to what you are now." Her face, her eyes, her whole body expressed the admiration she felt for his powers.

There was a little silence; then he said gravely, "If I could only persuade myself that it was possible that a girl of your age could love a man of mine—" Lydia caught her underlip in a white tooth—she had not meant love—she had not thought it a question of that. His sensitive egotism understood her thought without any spoken word, and he added, "And I should be content with nothing else—nothing else, Lydia."

In all her cogitation on the possibility of her marriage with the governor she had somehow never thought of his expecting her to love him—to be in love with him.

She walked on a few steps, and then said, "I don't think I shall ever be in love—I never have. I feel for you a more serious respect and admiration than I have ever felt for anyone, man or woman."

"And what do you feel for this little blond whippersnapper who is always under your feet?"

"For Bobby?" Her surprise was genuine that his name should be dragged into a serious discussion. "I feel affection for Bobby. He is very useful and kind. I could never love him. Oh, mercy no!"

"Do you mean to say," said Albee, "you have never felt—you

have never had a man take you in his arms, and say to yourself as he did, 'This is living'?"

"No, no, no, no! Never, never!" said Lydia. She lied passionately, so passionately that she never stopped to remember that she was lying. "I don't want to feel like that. You don't understand me, governor. To feel what I feel for you is more, much more than—"

She stopped without finishing her sentence.

"You make me very proud, very happy when you talk like that," said Albee. "I certainly never expected that the happiest time of my life—these last few weeks—would come to me after I was fifty. I wonder," he added, turning and looking her over with a sort of paternal amusement which she had grown to like—"I wonder if there were really girls like you in my own time, if I had had sense enough to find them."

Lydia, who was under the impression that her whole future was being settled there and then in Potomac Park, within sight of the White House, on which she kept a metaphysical eye, felt that this was the ideal way for a man and woman to discuss their marriage—not coldly, but without surging waves of emotion to blind their eyes. Marriage had not been actually mentioned. Nothing definite had been said by either of them when before five they came in to join Benny at tea. But Lydia had no doubt of the significance of their talk. Like most clear-sighted heiresses, she know, rationally, that her fortune was a part of her charms; but like most human beings, she found it easy to believe that she was loved for herself.

They were to go back to New York on the midnight train so that the governor might be in time for his morning's work in the investigation, but before going he was having a small dinner party. An extra man for Benny, a distinguished member of the House, and the senator from his own state—an old political ally—and his wife. His wife had been a Washington woman of an old family, and now with her husband's money and position her house was a place of some political importance.

From the moment the Framinghams arrived a cloud began to descend on Lydia. She liked them both—the fresh-faced, white-haired, clever, wise senator and his pretty, elegant wife—elegant, but a little more elaborate than the same type in New York. Mrs. Framingham's hair was more carefully curled, her dress a trifle richer and tighter, her jewels more numerous than Lydia's or Miss Bennett's; but still Lydia recognized her at once as an equal—a woman who had her own way socially in her own setting.

She liked the Framinghams—it was Albee she liked less well. He was different from the instant of their entrance. To use the

60

language of the nursery, he began to show off, not in connection with his success of the morning—Lydia could have forgiven some vanity about that performance—but about social matters, the opera, Miss Thorne's box, and then—Lydia knew it was coming—the Pulsifers. He wanted Mrs. Framingham to know that he had been asked to the Pulsifers'. He did it this way:

"You may imagine, Mrs. Framingham, how much flattered I feel that Miss Thorne should have come on to the hearing, missing one of the most brilliant parties of the season—yes, the Pulsifers'. Of course, as far as I am concerned, it is a great relief to side-step that sort of thing. Oh, I don't wish to appear ungracious. It was very kind of Mrs. Pulsifer to invite me, but I was glad of an excuse to avoid it. Only for Miss Thorne—"

Even his voice sounded different—specious, servile—"servile" was the word in Lydia's mind. Mrs. Framingham, if she were impressed by the news that the governor could have gone if he had wanted, betrayed not the least interest. Lydia pieced out the story of her attitude to the governor. Evidently when she had been last in the capital of her husband's state Albee had been only a powerful member of the legislature—useful to her husband, but not invited to her house. All very well, thought Lydia—a criticism of Mrs. Framingham's lack of vision—if only Albee would stand by it, resent it, and not be so eager to please.

As she grew more and more silent the governor, ably seconded by Miss Bennett, grew more and more affable. It would have been a very pleasant party if Lydia had not been there. Miss Bennett could not imagine what was wrong; and even Albee, with his instinctive knowledge of human beings and his quick egotism to guide him, was too well pleased with his own relation to his party to feel anything wrong. Lydia's silence only gave him greater scope.

She did not see him alone again. After dinner they went to the theater and then to the train. In the compartment she and Benny had the little scene they always had on these occasions. Lydia assumed that she as the younger woman would take the upper berth. Miss Bennett asserted that she infinitely preferred it. Lydia ignored the assertion, doubting its accuracy. Miss Bennett insisted, and Lydia yielded—yielded largely for the reason that the dispute seemed to her undignified.

She was glad on this occasion that she was in the lower berth, for she did not sleep, and raising the shade she stared out. There was something soothing in lying back on her pillows watching the world flash past you as if you were being dragged along on a magic carpet while everyone else slept.

Her future was all in chaos again. She could never marry

61

Albee. She thought, as she so often did, of Ilseboro's parting words about her being such a bully that she would always get second-rate playmates. It seemed to her the real trouble lay in her demand that they should be first-rate. Most women would have accepted Albee as first-rate, but she knew he wasn't. She felt tragically alone.

Their train got in at seven, and as soon as Lydia had had a bath and breakfast—that is, by nine o'clock—she was calling Eleanor on the telephone. Consideration of the fact that her friend might have been up late the night before was not characteristic of Lydia. Tragic or not, she was curious to hear what had happened at the Pulsifers'. She wanted Eleanor to come and lunch with her. No, Miss Bellington was going back to the country that morning. It was finally settled that Lydia should drive Eleanor home in the little runabout and stay for luncheon with her.

It was one of those mild days that make you think March is really a spring month. Eleanor did not like to drive fast; and Lydia, with unusual thoughtfulness, remembered her friend's wishes and drove at a moderate pace. That was one way to tell if Lydia was really fond of anyone—if she showed the sort of consideration that most people are brought up to show to all human beings. The two women gossiped like schoolgirls.

"Was Bobby too wonderful in his costume?"

"My dear, I wish you could have seen him. May Swayne made really rather a goose of herself about him."

"Yes"—this thoughtfully from Lydia—"she always does when I'm not there to protect him. And Fanny—was her Cleopatra as comic as it sounded?"

Eleanor wanted to know about Lydia's experiences—the hearing, Washington. Lydia told how magnificently the governor had defended himself, and added nothing at first about the less desirable aspects of his character. She thought this reserve arose from loyalty, but the fact that the governor was generally considered to be her own property made her feel that to criticize him was to cheapen her own assets. But she had great confidence in Eleanor, and by the time they had sat down to lunch alone together she found herself launched on the whole story of the impression Albee had made upon her. So interested, indeed, was she in the narrative that when toward the end of luncheon Eleanor was called to the telephone she hardly noticed the incident, except as it was an interruption. She sat going over it all in her mind during the few minutes that Eleanor was away, and the instant Eleanor came back she resumed what she was saying.

Eleanor was a satisfactory listener. She did not begin scolding you, telling you what you ought to have done before you had half finished. She did not allow herself to be reminded of adventures of her own and snatch the narrative away from you. She sat silent but alert, conveying by something neither words nor motion that she followed every intricacy.

Her comment was, "I feel rather sorry for Albee."

"You mean you don't think he's a worm?" Lydia was genuinely surprised.

"Oh, yes, I think he is just as you represent him! I feel sorry for people whose faults make them comic and defenseless. After all, Albee has great abilities. You don't care a bit for those, because he turns out not to be perfect. And who are you, my dear, to demand perfection?"

"I don't! I don't," cried Lydia eagerly. "Oh, Eleanor, men are fortunate! Apparently they can fall in love without a bit respecting you—all the more if they don't—but a woman must believe a man has something superior about him, if it is only his wickedness. I don't demand perfection—not a bit—but I do ask that a man's faults should not be contemptible faults; that he should have some force and snap; that he should be at least a man."

"That doesn't seem to please you always either."

"You're thinking of Ilseboro. I did like Ilseboro, though he was such a bully."

"No, I was thinking of Dan."

Lydia opened her eyes as if she couldn't imagine whom she meant.

"Of Dan?"

"Dan O'Bannon."

"Oh, it's got as far as being 'Dan' now, has it?"

"You dislike him for these very qualities you say you demand," Eleanor went on—"force and strength—"

Lydia broke in.

"Strength and force! What I really dislike about him, Eleanor dear, is that you take him so seriously. I can't bear to see you making yourself ridiculous about any man."

"I don't feel I make myself ridiculous, thank you."

"I don't mean you'd ever be undignified, but it is ridiculous for a woman of your attainment and position to take that young Irishman so seriously—a country lawyer. Why, I can't bear to name you in the same breath!"

Eleanor raised her shoulders a little.

"He'll be here in a few minutes."

"Here?" Lydia sprang up. "I'm off then!"

"I wish you wouldn't go. If you saw more of him you'd change your opinion of him."

63

"If I saw more of him I'd insult him. Send for my car, will you? No, no, Eleanor! I know I'm right about this—really, I am. Some day you'll come to agree with me."

"Or you with me," answered Eleanor, but she rang and ordered Lydia's car.

A few minutes later Lydia was on her way home. It was a day when everything had gone wrong, she thought; but now a cure for the nerves was open to her. The roads were empty at that hour, and her foot pressed the accelerator. She thought that if Eleanor married O'Bannon she would lose her. She would like to prevent it. With most girls she could poison their minds against a man by representing him as ludicrous, but Eleanor was not easily swayed. Lydia wondered if after they were married she could be more successful. She had never hated anyone quite the way she hated O'Bannon. It was fun, in a way, to hate a person. Her spirits began to mount as speed, like a narcotic, soothed her nerves. The road was smooth and new and had stood the winter frosts well. The first spring thaw had deposited on its cement surface a dampness which glistened here and there and made the wheels slip and the car waver like a living thing. This only increased Lydia's pleasure and fixed her attention as on the narrow ribbon of cement she passed an occasional car.

Suddenly as she dashed past a crossroad she caught a glimpse of a motorcycle and a khaki figure already preparing to mount. She turned her head far enough to be sure that it was the same man. She saw him hold up his hand, heard his voice calling to her to stop.

"No more bracelets, my friend," she thought, and her car shot forward faster than ever.

She fancied that he must be having trouble getting his engine started, for she did not hear the motorcycle behind her. She knew that just before she entered the village about half a mile ahead of her there was an unfrequented little road that ran into the highroad she was on, almost parallel to it. If she could get on that she could let the car out for miles and miles. The only trouble was that she would have to turn almost completely round and, going at this pace, that wouldn't be easy.

Presently she caught the sound of the quick, regular explosion, and the anticipated speck appeared in her mirror. All her powers were concentrated now on keeping her car straight on the slippery road, but she thought grimly, "Worse for him on two wheels than for me on four." She felt a mounting determination not to be caught—a willingness to take any risk. Still the man on the motorcycle was gaining on her. At an inequality in the road her front wheels veered sharply. With a quick twist she recovered

64

control and went straight again. She knew how to drive, thank goodness!

With the man gaining on her, she welcomed the sight of her back road coming in on the right. Even at the pace she could get round it, she thought, by skidding her car; and the motorcycle couldn't but would shoot ahead right into the village of Wide Plains, scattering children and dogs before him as he came. She felt a wild amusement at the thought, but her face did not relax its tense sternness.

She tightened her grip on the wheel, working the car to the left, preparing for the turn, and put on her brakes hard enough to lock the back wheels, expecting to feel the quick sideways slip of a skidding car. Instead there was a terrific impact—the crash of steel and glass, a cry. Her own car shot out of her control, turning a complete circle, bounded off the road and on again, and came slowly to a standstill, pointing in the same direction as before, but some yards beyond the fork in the road. She looked about her. Fragments of the motorcycle were strewn from the corner to where in a ditch at the foot of a telegraph pole the man was lying, a featureless mass.

She leaped out of her car. Amid the wreckage of the motorcycle the clock stared up at her like a little white face. The world seemed to have become silent; her feet beating on the cement as she ran made the only sound. The man lay motionless. He was bent together and strangely twisted like a boneless scarecrow thrown down by the winds. An arm was under him, his eyes were closed, blood was oozing from his mouth. She stooped over him, trying to lift his body into a more natural position; but he was a large man, and she could do nothing with him. She looked up from the struggle and found to her astonishment that she was no longer alone. People seemed to have sprung from the earth, the air was full of screams and explanations. A large touring car had come to a standstill near by. She vaguely remembered having passed it. A flivver was panting across the road. Everyone was asking questions, which she did not stop to answer. The important thing was to get the man into the touring car and take him to the hospital.

She was so absorbed in all his that her own connection with the situation did not enter her mind. As she sat in the back of the car supporting his body, the blood stiffening on her own dark clothes, she thought only of her victim. She was not the type of egotist who thinks always, "How terrible that this should have happened to me!"

She said to herself: "He probably has a wife and children. It would have been better if I had been the one to be killed."

Arrived at the hospital, she followed him into the ward where the stretcher carried him, and waited outside the screen while the nurses cut his clothes off. It seemed to her hours before the young house surgeon emerged, shaking his head.

"Fracture of the base," he said. "If he gets through the next twenty-four hours he'll have a 60 per cent chance," and he hurried away to telephone the details to his chief.

As she sat there she realized that her own body was sore and stiff. She must have wrenched herself, or struck the steering wheel in the sudden turn of the car. She felt suddenly exhausted. There seemed no point in waiting. They could telephone her the result of the night. She left her name and address and went home by train.

She made a vow to herself that she would never drive a car again. She would not explain it or discuss it, but nothing should ever induce her to touch a steering wheel. It was an inadequate expiation. Every time she shut her eyes she saw that heap of blood and steel at the foot of the telegraph pole. Oh, if time could only be turned back so that she could be starting a second time from Eleanor's door! It never crossed her mind that this terrible personal misfortune which had befallen her made her seriously amenable to the law.

CHAPTER VIII

Drummond died late in the evening. An account of the accident was in the headlines of the morning papers. Unfortunately for Lydia, he was a conspicuous local figure. He had had the early popularity of a good-looking, dissipated boy, and then he had been one of the men who had not waited for the draft but had volunteered and gone into the Regular Army, and had come home from France unwounded, with a heroic record. Moreover, there had been a long boy-and-girl love affair between him and Alma Wooley, the daughter of the hardware merchant. Mr. Wooley, who was a native Long Islander, hard and wise, had been opposed to the engagement until, after the war, the return of Drummond as a hero made opposition impossible. It was at this point that O'Bannon had come to the rescue, securing the position of traffic policeman for the young man. The marriage was to have taken place in June.

Before Drummond died he recovered consciousness long enough to recognize the pale girl at his beside and to make an ante-mortem statement as to the circumstances of the accident.

Eleanor heard of the accident in the evening, but did not know of Drummond's death until early the following morning. She called up O'Bannon, but he had already left his house. At the office she was asked if Mr. Foster would do. Mr. Foster would not do. With her clear mind and recently acquired knowledge of criminal law, she knew the situation was serious. She called up Fanny Piers and found she was spending the day in town. Noel came to the telephone. He was very casual.

"Yes, poor Lydia," he said; "uncomfortable sort of thing to have happened to you."

"Rather more than uncomfortable," answered Eleanor. "Do you know if she's been arrested?"

Piers laughed over the telephone. Of course she hadn't been. Really, his tone seemed to say, Eleanor allowed her socialistic ideas to run away with her judgment. Poor Lydia hadn't meant any harm—it was the sort of thing that might happen to anyone. Oh, they might try her—as a matter of form. But what could they do to her?

"Well," said Eleanor, "people have been known to go to prison for killing someone on the highway."

Piers agreed as if her point was irrelevant.

"Oh, yes, some of those careless chauffeurs. But a thing like this is always arranged. You'll see. You couldn't get a grand jury to indict a girl like Lydia. It will be arranged."

"Arranged," thought Eleanor as she hung up the receiver, "only at the expense of Dan O'Bannon's honor or career."

She did not want that, and yet she did want to help Lydia. She felt deeply concerned for the girl, more aware than usual of her warm, honest affection for her. She often thought of Lydia as she had appeared on her first day at school. The head mistress had brought her into the study and introduced her to the teacher in charge. All the girls had looked up and stared at the small, black-eyed new pupil with the bobbed hair and slim legs in black silk stockings, one of which she was cleverly twisting about the other. She was shy and monosyllabic, utterly unused to children of her own age; and yet even then she had shown a certain capacity for comradeship, for under the elbows of the two tall teachers she had directed a slow, shy smile at the girls as much as to say, "Wait till we get together! We'll fix them!"

She was very well turned out, for Miss Bennett had just taken charge, but not so well equipped mentally, the long succession of her governesses having each spent more time in destroying the teachings of her predecessors than in making progress on her own account. Much to Lydia's chagrin, she was put in a class of children younger than she.

This was shortly before Christmas. Before the second term she had managed to get herself transferred into a class of her contemporaries. She had never studied before, because in old times it had seemed to her the highest achievement lay in thwarting her governesses. But the instant it became desirable to attain knowledge she found no difficulty in attaining it. It had amused her studying late into the night when Miss Bennett thought she was asleep.

In the same way she had decided to make a friend of Eleanor, who was a class above her and prominent in school life. There had been nothing sentimental about the friendship. She had admired Eleanor's clear mind and moral courage then, just as she admired them now.

It was of that little girl twisting one leg about the other that Eleanor thought now with a warm affection that the later Lydia had not destroyed. She ordered her car and drove into town to the Thorne house. At the door Morson betrayed just the proper solemnity—the proper additional solemnity—for he was never gay.

Yes, Miss Thorne was in, but he could not be sure that she could see Miss Bellington at the moment. Mr. Wiley was in the drawing-room.

"Mr. Wiley?" said Eleanor, trying to remember.

"The lawyer, madam."

Eleanor hesitated.

"Tell her I'm here," she said, and presently Morson came back and conducted her to the drawing-room.

Lydia's drawing-room was brilliant with vermilion lacquer, jade, rock crystal, a Chinese painting or two and huge cushioned armchairs and sofas. Here she and Miss Bennett and Mr. Wiley were sitting—at least Mr. Wiley and Miss Bennett were sitting, and Lydia was standing, playing with a jade dog from the mantelpiece, pressing its cold surface against her cheek.

As Eleanor entered, Lydia, with hardly a sound, did a thing she had occasionally seen her do before—she suddenly seemed to radiate greeting and love and gratitude. Miss Bennett introduced Mr. Wiley.

Wiley had established his position early in life—early for a lawyer; so now at fifty-eight he had thirty years of crowded practice behind him. In the nineties, a young man of thirty, his slim frock-coated figure, his narrow, fine features and dark, heavy mustache were familiar in most important court cases, and in the published accounts of them his name always had a prominent place. His enemies at one time had been contemptuous of his legal profundity and had said that he was more of an actor than a lawyer; but if so juries seemed to be more swayed by art than law, for Wiley had a wonderful record of successes. He was a man of scrupulous financial integrity—universally desired as a trustee—an honorable gentleman, a leader at the bar. It was hard to see how Lydia could be in better hands. He might not have been willing to undertake her case but for the fact that he had been her father's lawyer and was her trustee. He had a thorough familiarity, attained through years of conflict over finances, with all the problems of his client's disposition. He knew, for instance, that she would be absolutely truthful with him, a knowledge a lawyer so rarely has in regard to his clients. He knew, too, that she might carry this quality into the witness chair and might ruin her own case with the jury. He was a man accustomed to being listened to, and he was being listened to now.

Eleanor sat down, saying she was sorry if she interrupted them. She didn't. Wiley drew her in and made her feel one of the conference.

"I had really finished what I was saying," he added.

"I only wanted to know if the situation were serious," said Eleanor.

"Serious, Miss Bellington?" Wiley looked at her seriously. "To kill a human being while violating the law?"

"Mr. Wiley considers it entirely a question of how the case is

69

managed," said Lydia. There was not a trace of amusement in her tone or her expression.

"To be absolutely candid," Wiley continued, "and Lydia tells me she wants the facts, I should say that if juries were normal, impartial, unemotional people Lydia would be found guilty of manslaughter in the second degree—on her own story. Fortunately, however, the collective intelligence of a jury is low; and skillfully managed, the case of a beautiful young orphan may be made very appealing, very pathetic."

"Pathos has never been my strong point," observed Lydia.

"The great danger is her own attitude," said Miss Bennett to Eleanor. "She doesn't seem to care whether she's convicted or not."

Lydia moved her shoulders with a gesture that confirmed Miss Bennett's impression, and then suddenly turned.

"I don't believe you want me for a few minutes, Mr. Wiley. I want to speak to Eleanor."

She dragged her friend away with her to her own little sitting room upstairs. Here her calm disappeared.

"Aren't lawyers terrible, Eleanor? Here I am—I've killed a man! Why shouldn't I go to prison? I'm not quixotic. I didn't want to be convicted, but Wiley shocks me, assuming that I can't be because I'm a woman and rich and he can play on the jury."

"I should not say that he assumed that you were safe, Lydia."

"Oh, yes, he does! Don't be like Benny. She sees me in stripes at once. What Wiley means is that as long as I am fortunate enough to have the benefit of his services I'm perfectly safe, not because I did not mean to kill Drummond, but because he, Wiley, will make the jury cry over me. Isn't that disgusting?"

"Yes, it is," said Eleanor.

"Oh, Eleanor, you are such a comfort!" said Lydia, and began to cry. Eleanor had never seen her cry before. She did it very gently, without sobs, and after a few minutes controlled herself again, and tucked away her handkerchief and said, "Do you think everyone would hate to have a car that had killed someone! I shall never drive again, and yet I couldn't sell it—couldn't take money for it. Will you accept it, Eleanor? You wouldn't have to drive the way I did, you know."

Eleanor, pleading the shortness of her sight, declined the car.

"You ought to go back and talk to Mr. Wiley, my dear."

Lydia shrugged her shoulders.

"I don't care much what happens to me," she said.

Eleanor hesitated. She saw suddenly that what she was about to say was the principal object of her visit.

70

"Lydia, I hope that you will come out all right, but you don't know Dan O'Bannon as I do, and—"

"You think he will want to convict me?"

"Not you personally, of course. But he believes in the law. He wants to believe in its honesty and equality. He suffered last month, I know, in convicting a delivery-wagon driver, and his offense wasn't half as flagrant as yours. Oh, Lydia, have some imagination! Don't you see that his own honor and democracy will make him feel it more his duty to convict you than all the less conspicuous criminals put together?"

A strange change had taken place in Lydia during this speech. At the beginning of it she had been shrunk into a corner of a deep chair; but as Eleanor spoke life seemed to be breathed into her, until she sat erect, grew tense, and finally rose to her feet.

"You mean there would be publicity, political advantage, in sending a person in my position to prison?"

"Don't be perverse, Lydia. I mean that, more than most men, he will see his duty is to treat you as he would any criminal. You make it difficult for me to tell you something that I must tell you. Mr. O'Bannon feels, I'm afraid, a certain amount of antagonism toward you."

A staring, insolent silence was Lydia's answer.

Eleanor went on: "Do you remember after dinner at the Piers' you told me about the policeman you had bribed? You asked me not to tell, but I'm sorry—I can't tell you how sorry—that I did tell. I told Dan. I would give a good deal if I hadn't, but—"

"My dear," Lydia laughed, but without friendliness, "don't distress yourself. What difference does it make? I nearly told him myself."

"It makes a great deal of difference. It made him furious against you. He felt you were debauching a young man trying to do his duty."

"What a prig you make that man out, Eleanor! But what of it?"

"I got an impression, Lydia—I don't know how—that it turned him against you; that he will be less inclined to be pitiful."

"Pitiful!" cried Lydia. "Since when have I asked Dan O'Bannon for pity? Let him do his duty, and my lawyers will do theirs; and let me tell you, Eleanor, you and he will be disappointed in the results."

Eleanor said firmly, "I think you must take back that 'you,' Lydia."

Lydia shrugged her shoulders.

"Well, you say your friend wants to convict me, and you want your friend to succeed, I suppose. That is success for him, getting people to prison, isn't it?" She began this in one of her most

71

irritating tones; and then she suddenly repented and, putting her hand on Eleanor's shoulder, she added, "Eleanor, I'm all on edge. Thank you a lot for coming. I think I will go back and tell what you've said to old Wiley."

Eleanor waited to telephone to Fanny Piers and Mrs. Pulsifer, knowing it would be wise to create a little favorable public opinion. As she went downstairs the drawing-room door opened and Miss Bennett came softly out, shutting the door carefully behind her.

"Thank heaven for you, Eleanor!" she said. "You have certainly worked a miracle." Eleanor looked uncomprehending, and she went on: "At first she was so naughty to poor Mr. Wiley—would hardly discuss the case at all; but now since you've talked to her she is quite different. She has even consented to send for Governor Albee—the obvious thing, with his friendship and political power."

Eleanor's shoulders were rather high anyhow, and when she drew them together she looked like a wooden soldier. She did it now as she said with distaste, "But is this a question of politics?"

"My dear, you know the district attorney is a political officer, and they say this young man is extremely ambitious. Certainly he would listen—he'd have to—to a man at the head of the party like Albee. I feel much easier in my mind. The governor can do anything, and now that Lydia has come to her senses she is determined to go into court with the best case possible, and you know how clever she is. Thank you, Eleanor, for all you have done for us."

Like many workers of miracles, Eleanor went away surprised at her own powers. The idea of O'Bannon being coerced or rewarded into letting Lydia off gave her exquisite pain. She felt like warning him to do his duty, even if it meant Lydia's being found guilty. Yet she sincerely wanted Lydia saved—meant to go as far as she could to save her. She knew with what a perfect surface of honesty such things could be done; how a district attorney, while from the public's point of view prosecuting a case with the utmost vigor, might leave open some wonderful technical escape for the defense. It could be done without O'Bannon losing an atom of public respect. But she, Eleanor, would know; would know as she saw him conducting the case; would know when a year or so later, after everyone else had forgotten, he would receive his reward—some political appointment or perhaps a financial chairmanship. Albee had great powers in business as well as politics. In her own mind she formulated the words, "I have the utmost confidence in O'Bannon." But she knew, too, how all people of passionate, quick temperaments are sometimes swept by their own desires, and how easily most lawyers could find rational grounds for taking the position they desired to take. It would be so natural for any man under the plea of pity for a young woman like Lydia to allow himself to be subtly corrupted into letting her off.

Eleanor's own position was not simple. She faced it clearly. She was for Lydia, whatever happened, as far as her conduct went; but in spite of herself her sympathies swung to and fro. When women like Fanny Piers and May Swayne said, with a certain relish they couldn't keep out of their tones and reluctant dimples at the corners of their mouths, "Isn't this too dreadful about poor Lydia?" then she was whole-heartedly Lydia's. But when she detected in all her friends—except Bobby, who was frankly frightened—the belief that they were beyond the law, that nothing could happen to any member of their protected group, then she felt she would enjoy nothing so much as seeing one of them prove an exception to the general immunity.

The coroner held Lydia for the grand jury in ten thousand dollars' bail. This had been considered a foregone conclusion and did not particularly distress or alarm Eleanor. What did alarm her was her inability to get in touch with O'Bannon. In all the months of their quick, intimate friendship this had never happened before. Press of business had never kept him entirely away. Now she could not even get him to come to the telephone.

She was not the only person who was attempting to see him on Lydia's behalf. Bobby Dorset had made several efforts, and finally caught him between the courthouse and his office. Bobby took the tone that the whole thing was fantastic; that O'Bannon was too much of a gentleman to send any girl to prison, irritating the man he had come to placate by something frivolous and unreal in his manner—the only manner Bobby knew.

And then as Lydia's case grew darker Albee came. O'Bannon was in his study at home, the low-ceilinged room opening off the dining room. It had a great flat baize-covered desk, and low open shelves running round the walls, containing not only law books, but novels and early favorites—Henty and Lorna Doone and many records of travel and adventure.

Here he was sitting, supposed to be at work on the Thorne case, about nine o'clock in the evening. Certainly his mind was occupied with it and the papers were laid out before him. He was going over and over, the same treadmill that his mind had been chained to ever since he had stood by Drummond's bedside with Alma Wooley clinging, weeping, to his hand.

Lydia Thorne had committed a crime, and his duty was to present the case against the criminal. Sometimes of course a district attorney was justified in taking into consideration extenuating circumstances which could not always be brought out in court. But

73

in this case there were no extenuating circumstances. Every circumstance he knew was against her. Her character was harsh and arrogant. She had already violated the law in bribing Drummond. First she had corrupted the poor boy, and then she had killed him. She deserved punishment more than most of the criminals who came into his court, and his duty was to present the case against her. He repeated it over and over to himself. Why, he was half a crook to consider this case as different from any other case—and if she did get off she wouldn't be grateful. She'd just assume that there had not been and never could be any question of convicting a woman like herself. He remembered her bending to look at him under the candle shades of the Piers' dinner table and announcing her disbelief in the equal administration of the laws. But yet, if she should come to him—if she would only come to him, pleading for herself as she had once for a few minutes pleaded for Evans—He could almost see her there in the circle of his reading light, close to him—could almost smell the perfume of violets.

"I hope to God she doesn't come," he said to himself, and desired it more than anything in life.

At that very moment the doorbell rang. O'Bannon's heart began to beat till it hurt him. If she were there he must see her, and if he saw her he must again take her in his arms, and if—it was his duty to present the case against her.

There was a knock on his door, and his mother entered ushering in Governor Albee. Great and wise men came from East and West to see her son, her manner seemed to say.

"Well, O'Bannon," said the governor, "I haven't seen you since—let me see—the 1916 convention, wasn't it?"

The younger man pulled himself together. He was not a politician for nothing, and he had control, almost automatically, of a simple, friendly manner.

"But I've seen you, governor," he answered. "I went in the other day to hear your cross-examination on that privileged-communication point. I learned a lot. We're all infants compared with you when it comes to that sort of thing."

"Oh"—Albee gave one of his straight-armed waves of the band—"everyone tells me you have your own method of getting the facts. I hear very fine things of you, O'Bannon. There's an impression that Princess County will soon be looking for another district attorney."

Mrs. O'Bannon stole reluctantly away, closing the door behind her. The two men went on flattering each other, as each might have flattered a woman. Both were now aware that a serious situation was before them. They began to talk of the great party to which they

74

belonged. The governor mentioned his personal responsibility—by which he meant his personal power—as a national committeeman. He spoke of an interview with the leader of the party in New York— the purveyor of great positions.

"He's going to put the chairmanship of this new commission up to me. It's not so much financially—seventy-five hundred—but the opportunity, the reputation a fellow might make. It needs a big man, and yet a young one. I'm for putting in a young man."

That was all. The governor began after that to speak of his coming campaign for the Senate, but O'Bannon knew now exactly why he had come. He had come to offer him a bribe. It was not the first time he had been offered a bribe. He remembered a family of Italians who had come to him frankly with all their savings in a sincere belief that that was the only way to save a son and brother. They had gone away utterly unable to understand why their offering had been rejected, but with a confused impression that district attorneys in America came too high for them. He had not felt any anger against their simple effort at corruption—only pity; but a sudden furious anger swept him against Albee, so smooth, so self-satisfied. Unanalytic, like most hot-blooded people—who in the tumult of their emotions are too much occupied to analyze and when the tumult ceases are unable to believe it ever existed— O'Bannon did not understand the sequence of his emotions. For an instant he was angry, and then he felt a sort of desperate relief. At least the question of his attitude in the case was settled. Now he must prosecute to the utmost of his ability. One couldn't let a sleek, crooked old politician go through the world thinking that he had bribed you—one couldn't be bribed.

He leaned his brow on his hand, shielding his whole face from the light, while he drew patterns on the blotting paper with a dry pen. The governor broke off with an appearance of spontaneity.

"But I mustn't run on like this about my own affairs," he said. "I came, as perhaps you guessed, about this unfortunate affair of poor Miss Thorne. I don't know if you know her personally—"

He paused. He really could not remember. He believed Lydia had mentioned having seen the man somewhere.

"I've met her once or twice," said O'Bannon.

"Well, if you've seen her you know that she's a rare and beautiful creature; but if you don't know her you don't know how sensitive she is; sheltered and proud; doesn't show her deep, human feelings."

A slight movement of the district attorney's hand brought his mouth and chin into the area of illumination. Their expression was not agreeable.

"No," he said, "I must own I did not get all that."

"This whole thing is almost killing her," Albee went on. "Really I believe that if she has to go into court—well, of course she must go into court, poor child, and hear it all gone over and over before a jury. Imagine how anyone—you or I would feel if we had killed a man, and then add a young woman's natural sensitiveness and pity. You can guess what she is going through. I've sat with her for hours. It's pitiful—simply pitiful. Anything you can do, O'Bannon, that will make it easier for her I shall take as a personal favor to me, a favor I shall never forget, believe me."

The governor smiled his human, all-embracing smile, almost like a priest. There was a moment's silence. Albee's experience was that there usually was a moment while the idea sank in.

Then the younger man asked with great deliberation, "Just what is your interest in this case, Governor Albee?"

Perfectly calm himself, Albee noted with some amusement the strain in the other's tone. He had expected the question—a natural one. It was natural the fellow should wish to be assured that the favor he was about to do was a real one, a substantial one, something that would be remembered. He would be taking a certain chance, considering the newspaper interest and all the local resentment over the case. Reëlection might be rendered impossible. Albee thought to himself that Lydia would forgive a slight exaggeration of the bond between them if that exaggeration served to set her free.

"Well, that's rather an intimate question, Mister District Attorney," he said. "To most people I should answer that she is a lady whom I esteem and admire; but to you—in strictest confidence—I don't mind saying that I have every hope and expectation of making her my wife." And he added less solemnly, "What are you young fellows thinking of to let an old man like me get ahead of you, eh?" Bending forward he slapped the other man on the shoulder.

O'Bannon stood up as if a mighty hand had reached from the ceiling and pulled him upright. The action was all that was left of the primitive impulse to wring Albee's neck.

"There is nothing I can do to help Miss Thorne," he said. "You know enough about criminal procedure to know that. The case against her is very strong."

"Oh, very strong—in the newspapers," said the governor with another of his waves of his hand. "But you mustn't let your cases be tried in the newspapers. I always made it a rule never to let the newspapers influence me in a case."

"I have a better rule than that," said the other. "I don't let anything influence me except the facts in the case." He was still standing, and Albee now rose too.

"I see," he said, not quite so suavely as before. "You mean you go ahead your own way and don't mind making enemies."

"I sometimes like it," answered O'Bannon.

"Making them is all right." Albee looked right at him. "Taking the consequences of doing so isn't always so enjoyable. Good night."

When the sound of the governor's motor had died away O'Bannon went back to his desk. His mother had long ago gone upstairs, and the house was quiet. Disgust and anger were like a poison in his veins. So that vile, sleek old man was to have her? Love was out of the question? She did not even have the excuse of needing money! What a loathsome bargain! What a loathsome woman! To think he had allowed himself to be stirred by her beauty? He wouldn't touch her with his little finger now if she were the last woman in the world. Albee? Good God! There must be thirty-five years between them. Someone ought to stop it. She would be better in prison than giving herself to an old man like that. She was no ignorant child. She knew what she was doing. If he were the girl's brother or father he'd rather see her dead.

It was after midnight when he set to work on the papers in the case. He worked all night. The old servant bringing Mrs. O'Bannon her breakfast in the early morning reported Mr. Dan as being up and away. He had come into the kitchen at six for a cup of coffee, his face as white as that sheet and his eyes nearly out of his head.

This was the afternoon that Eleanor selected to take the matter into her own hands and come to his office. She came late in the afternoon. It was after six. She saw his car standing in the street and she knew he was still there. She went in past the side entrance to Mr. Wooley's shop, up the worn wooden stairs, through the glass door with its gold letters, "Office of the District Attorney of Princess County." The stenographers and secretaries had gone. Their desks were empty, their typewriters hooded. O'Bannon was standing alone in the middle of the room with his hat and overcoat on, as if he had been caught by some disagreeable thought just in the moment of departure.

Eleanor's step made no sound on the stairs. He looked up in surprise as she opened the door, and as their eyes met she knew clearly that he did not want to see her. There was something almost brutal in the way that he looked at her and then looked away again, as if he hoped she might be gone when he looked back. If she had come on her own business she would have gone. As it was, she couldn't. She came in, and closing the door behind her she leaned against the handle.

"I'm sorry to bother you, Dan," she said, "but I must talk to you about Lydia Thorne."

"Miss Thorne's friends are doing everything they can to prevent the preparation of a case against her. They take all my time in interviews," he answered.

"Who else has been here?" asked Eleanor with a sinking heart.

"Oh, Bobby Dorset has been here. That interview was brief."

"And Governor Albee?"

O'Bannon looked at her with eyes that suddenly flared up like torches.

"Yes, the old fox," he said.

There was a pause during which Eleanor did not say a word, but her whole being, body and mind, was a question; and O'Bannon, though he had become this strange, hostile creature, was yet enough her old friend to answer it.

"If you have any influence with Miss Thorne tell her to keep politics out of it—to get a good lawyer and to prepare a good case."

Eleanor saw that Albee's mission had failed. She would have rejoiced at this, except that the hostility of O'Bannon's manner hurt her beyond the power of rejoicing. She was not like Lydia—stimulated by enmity. She felt wounded and chilled by it. She told herself, as women always do in these circumstances, that there was nothing personal about his attitude, but there was something terribly personal in her not being able to change his black mood.

"She has a good lawyer—Wiley. Who can be better than Wiley?" she asked.

"He's often successful, I believe."

He began snapping out the light over the desk—a hint not too subtle. Eleanor started twice to say that most people believed that no jury would convict a girl like Lydia, but every phrase she thought of sounded like a challenge. They went downstairs. Ordinarily he would have offered to drive her home, although her own car was waiting for her. Now he took off his soft hat and was actually turning away when she caught him by the sleeve. His arm remained limp, almost humanly sulky, in her grasp.

"I've never known you like this before, Dan," she said.

"You must do me the justice to say," he answered, "that lately I have done my best to keep out of your way."

Eleanor dropped his arm and he started to move away.

"Tell me one thing," she said. "The grand jury will indict her?"

"It will."

She nodded.

"That is what Mr. Wiley thinks."

78

"And he also thinks, I suppose," said O'Bannon, "that no jury will convict her?"

"And what do you think?"

"I think," he answered, so slowly that each word fell clearly, "that a conviction can be had and that I shall get it."

Eleanor did not answer. The chauffeur was holding open the door of her car, and she walked forward and got into it. She had learned the thing she had come to learn—a knowledge that the stand he took was an honorable one. She was glad that his hands were clean, but in her left side her heart ached like a tooth. He seemed a stranger to her—unfriendly, remote, remote as a man struggling in a whirlpool would be remote from even the friendliest spectator on the bank.

A few days later the grand jury found a true bill against Lydia. That was no surprise even to her friends. Wiley and Albee had both prepared her for that. The crime for which she was indicted, however, came as a shock. It was manslaughter in the first degree. Albee was, or affected to be, pleased. It proved they were bluffing, he said.

"It may cost you a little more on Wiley's bill," he said. "It costs a little more, I suppose, to be acquitted of manslaughter than of criminal negligence; but on the other hand it may save you a thousand-dollar fine. A jury might conceivably find you guilty of a crime for which you could be fined, but not of one for which the only punishment is imprisonment."

Bobby thought the indictment showed conclusively that there was some crooked work going on, and wanted the district attorney's office investigated. Most of Lydia's friends began to feel that this was really carrying the thing too far.

Thus New York.

In the neighborhood of Wide Plains it was generally known that O'Bannon and Foster were working early and late, and that the district attorney's office was out to get a conviction in the Thorne case.

CHAPTER IX

"Isaac Herrick."

"Here."

"William P. McCaw—I beg your pardon—McCann."

"Here."

"Royal B. Fisher. Mr. Fisher, you were not in court yesterday. Well, you did not answer the roll. Gentlemen, if you do not answer when your names are called I shall give your names to the court officer. Grover C. Wilbur."

"Here."

The county court room with its faded red carpet and shabby woodwork had the dignity of proportion which marks rooms built a hundred years ago under the solemn Georgian tradition.

Miss Bennett and Eleanor, guided by Judge Homans' secretary, came in through a side door, and passing the large American flag which hung above the judge's empty chair, they sat down in some cross seats on the left. Beyond the railing the room was already well filled with the new panel of jurors, the witnesses, the reporters and many of Lydia's friends, who were already jostling for places.

The clerk of the court, immediately in front of the judge's bench, but on a lower level, having finished calling the roll, was busily writing, writing, his well-brushed red-and-silver head bent so low over his great sheets that the small bare spot on top was presented to the court room. For one moment he and a tall attendant had become human and friendly over the fact that the counsel table was not on all fours, and the day before had rocked under the thundering fist of the lawyer in the last case. But as soon as it was stabilized with little wads of paper both men returned to their accustomed solemnity, the clerk to his lists and the attendant, standing erect at the railing, to viewing the unusual crowd and exclaiming at intervals "Find seats—sit down—find seats," which was, of course, just what everybody was trying to do.

Foster came in hurriedly with a stack of large manila envelopes in his hand. He bowed nervously to Miss Bennett and sat down just in front of her with his eyes fixed on the door.

The court stenographer came in and took his place, laid his neatly sharpened pencils beside his open book, yawned and threw his arm over the back of his chair. He seemed indifferent as to what story of human frailty was by means of his incredible facility about to be transferred to the records.

Yet he was not wholly without human curiosity, for presently he leaned over to the clerk and whispered, "What did the jury find in that abduction case?"

"Acquitted."

"Well, well!"

The two men exchanged a glance that betrayed that in their opinion jurors and criminals were pretty much on the same level.

A faint stir in the court, an anticipatory cry from the attendant of "Order, order," and Lydia and Wiley came in and sat down side by side at the corner of the long table—now perfectly steady. Lydia looked pale and severe. She had devoted a great deal of thought to her dress, not through vanity, but because dress was an element in winning her case. She was dressed as simply as possible, without being theatrically simple. She wore a dark serge and a black-winged hat. She nodded to Foster, smiled at Miss Bennett and Eleanor. She began looking coolly about her. She had never been in court, and the setting interested her. It was a good deal like a theater, she thought—the railed-off space represented the stage where all action was to take place, the judge's raised bench occupying the dominating position back center, the jury box on her right with its two tiers of seats, the witness chair on its high platform and between the judge and the jury. Close to the railing and at right angles to the jury box, the eight-foot-long counsel table, where she and Wiley had taken their places with their backs to the spectators outside the railing, were so exactly like a theatrical audience. Then a gavel beat sharply. Everyone stood up almost before being directed to do so, and Judge Homans came into court. He came slowly through the side door, his hands folded in front of him, his robes flowing about him, as a priest comes from the sacristy.

The judge, like the clerk, immediately became absorbed in writing. Foster sprang up and stood at his desk talking to him, but he never raised his head. Foster kept glancing over his shoulder at the door. Lydia knew for whom he was watching—like a puppy for its supper, she thought.

A voice rang out:

"The case of the People against Lydia Thorne. Lydia Thorne to the bar."

To Lydia the words suggested an elaborate game. She glanced at Miss Bennett, suppressing a smile, and saw that her companion's nerves were shaken by the sinister sound of them. Wiley rose.

"Ready—for the defense," he said.

Foster, with his eyes still on the door, murmured with less conviction, "Ready—for the people."

The clerk, laying aside his pen, had begun to take the names of the jurors out of the box at his elbow.

"Josiah Howell."

"Seat Number 1," echoed the attendant antiphonally.

"Thomas Peck."

"Seat Number 2."

Wiley, bending to Lydia's ear, whispered, "I want you to challenge freely—anyone you feel might be antagonistic. I trust to your woman's intuition. The jury is the important—"

She ceased to hear him, for she saw Foster's face light up and she knew that at last the district attorney was in court. She recognized his step behind her, and almost immediately his tall figure came within range of her vision. He sat down on the left next to Foster, crossed his arms, fixed his eyes on each juror who entered the box. It was to Lydia like the rising of the curtain on a great play.

"William McCann."

"Seat Number 12."

The jury was complete.

O'Bannon unfolded his long person and rose. Crossing the space in front of Lydia, he came and stood in front of the jury, looking from one to another, asking routine questions, but with a grave attention that made them seem spontaneous. Did any of them know the defendant or her counsel? Had any of them ever been arrested for speeding? Had anyone of them ever injured anyone with an automobile?

To Lydia his whole personality seemed different—more aggressive, more hostile. When, in speaking, he put out his fist she noticed the powerful bulk of his hand, the strength of his wrist. She could not see his face, for he stood with shoulder turned to her, but she could see the upturned faces of the jurors.

Number 10 was in the automobile business, and was excused. Number 2 admitted a slight acquaintance with the defendant, though Lydia couldn't remember him and was inclined to think he was merely escaping duty. Number 5, in the midst of the interrogation, suddenly volunteered the information that he was conscientiously opposed to capital punishment.

At this the judge looked up from his writing and said loudly, "But this isn't a capital-punishment case."

"No, no, I know," said Number 5 apologetically. "I just thought I'd mention it."

"Don't mention anything that has no bearing on the case," said the judge, and went back to his writing.

At noon, when the court adjourned, the jury was not yet satisfactory to the prosecution.

Lydia, Miss Bennett and Wiley drove over to Eleanor's for luncheon. Of the three women Lydia was the gayest.

"He really does—that man really does expect to put me behind bars," she said.

"The prospect apparently puts you in the highest spirits," said Eleanor.

Lydia laughed, showing her bright, regular little teeth.

"I do like a good fight," she answered.

That was the way she thought of it—as a personal struggle between the district attorney and herself. Since that first interview Wiley had no indifference to complain of. On the contrary, he complimented her on her grasp of the case—she ought to have been a lawyer. She had put every fact at his disposal—every fact that had any bearing on the case. She did not consider the exact nature of her former acquaintance with O'Bannon among these; that is to say, she mentioned that she had once met him at the Piers' and played bridge with him. She added that Eleanor felt he had taken a dislike to her. Wiley said nothing, but imagined that she might have played queen to a country attorney—irritating, of course.

About everything else, however, she went into details—especially about the bribing of Drummond, over which she apparently felt no shame at all. Both Albee and Wiley, who were often together in consultation with her, were horrified—not so much at her having done it as at her feeling no remorse. Wiley spoke as her lawyer. Albee, more human, more amused, shook his head.

"Really, my dear young lady, bribery of a police officer—"

"Oh, come, governor," said Lydia. "This from you!"

"I don't know what you mean. I never offered a man a bribe in all my life," said the governor earnestly.

"And exactly what did you say to Mr. O'Bannon in your recent interview?"

Wiley and Albee protested, more as if she were breaking the rules of a game than as if she were saying anything contrary to fact. Albee explained at some length that when a man was behaving wrongly through self-interest—which was, of course, what the district attorney was doing—it was perfectly permissible to show him that self-interest might lie along opposite lines. Lydia, unconvinced by this explanation, would do nothing but laugh annoyingly. At this both men turned on her, explaining that if the bracelet could be got in evidence, if it could be shown that she had bribed the man whom she later killed, the case would go against her.

"Oh, but they can't get it in," said Albee, "not unless you fall asleep, counselor, or the district attorney is an out-and-out crook."

Wiley, more cautious, wasn't so sure. If Lydia herself took the stand—

"Of course I shall testify in my own behalf," said Lydia.

"Yes," said Albee. "Exhibit A—a beautiful woman. Verdict—not guilty."

So the discussion always came back to the sympathy of the jury—the necessity of selecting the right twelve men. Nothing else was talked of during luncheon at Eleanor's that first day. Was Number 6 hostile? Did all farmers own automobiles nowadays? Number 1 was susceptible, Miss Bennett felt sure. He hadn't taken his eyes off Lydia. Number 7, on the contrary, was hypnotized, according to Lydia, by "that man."

By three o'clock the jury was declared satisfactory to the prosecution. It was Wiley's turn. His manner was very different from O'Bannon's—more conciliating. He seemed to woo the jury with what Lydia described in her own mind as a perfumed voice.

Number 2, in answer to Wiley's questions, admitted a prejudice against automobiles, since it was now impossible to drive his cows home along the highroad. He was excused.

Number 7, who had once owned a flourishing poultry farm, had been obliged to give it up.

"On account of motors?"

"Yes, and because it didn't pay."

Did he feel his prejudice was such as to prevent his rendering an impartial verdict in this case?

Number 7 looked blank and sulky, like a little boy stumped in class, and at last said it wouldn't.

"Excused," said Wiley.

"But I said it wouldn't," Number 7 protested.

"Excused," said Wiley, fluttering his hand.

Lydia had tapped twice on the table—the agreed signal.

By four o'clock the jury was satisfactory to both sides; and then, just as Lydia's nerves were tightened for the beginning of the great game, the court adjourned until ten o'clock the next morning. The judge, looking up from his writing, admonished the jury not to discuss the case with anyone, not even among themselves. The jurors produced unexpected hats and coats like a conjuring trick. The court attendant began shouting "Keep your seats until the jury has passed out," and the whole picture of the court dissolved.

Wiley was whispering to Lydia, "A very nice jury—a very intelligent, reasonable group of men." He rubbed his hands.

Lydia's eyes followed O'Bannon's back as he left the court with Foster trotting by his side.

84

"I wonder if the district attorney is equally pleased with them," she said.

Bobby Dorset drove back with them and stayed to dinner. Miss Bennett, who had a headache from the hot air and the effort of concentrating her mind, would have been glad to forget the trial, but Lydia and Bobby talked of nothing else. She kept a pad and pencil at hand to note down points that occurred to her. Bobby, with a mind at once acute and trivial, had collected odd bits of information—that the judge was hostile, that the door man said the verdict would be not guilty, and he had never been wrong in twenty-seven years.

Proceedings began the next morning by O'Bannon's opening for the prosecution. Lydia saw a new weapon directed against her that her advisers did not seem to appreciate—O'Bannon's terrible sincerity. His voice had not an artificial note in it. Meaning what he said, he was able to convince the jury.

"Gentlemen of the jury," he began, "the indictment in this case is manslaughter in the first degree. That is homicide without intent to effect death by a person committing or attempting to commit a misdemeanor. The People will show that on the eleventh day of March of this year the defendant, while operating an automobile on the highways of this county in a reckless and lawless manner, killed John Drummond, a traffic policeman, who was attempting to arrest her. Drummond, whose ante-mortem statement will be put in evidence—"

Suddenly Lydia's attention lapsed. This man who was trying to send her to prison had held her in his arms. She saw again the moon and the mist, and felt his firm hand on her shoulder. Memory seemed more real than this incredible reality. Then, just as steel doors shut on the red fire of a furnace, so her mind shut out this aspect of the situation, and she found she was listening—after how long a pause she did not know—to O'Bannon's words.

"—at the entrance to the village the road divides, the right fork turning back at an angle something less than a right angle. Round this corner the defendant attempted to go by a device known as skidding a car; that is to say, still going at a high rate of speed, she turned her wheels sharply to the right and put on her brakes hard enough to lock the back wheels."

"Yes, my friend," thought Lydia, "that's the way it's done. I wonder how many times you've skidded your own car to know so much about it."

"This procedure," O'Bannon's voice continued, "which is always a somewhat reckless performance, was in this case criminal. With the officer known to be overlapping her car on the left, she

85

might as well have picked up her car and struck him with it. Her car did so strike him, smashing his motorcycle to bits and causing the hideous injuries of which he died within a few hours."

Lydia closed her eyes. She saw that mass of bloodstained khaki and steel lying in the road and heard her own footsteps beating on the macadam.

"The People will prove that the defendant was committing a misdemeanor at the time. By Section 1950 of the Penal Law it is a misdemeanor to render the highways dangerous or to render a considerable number of persons insecure in life. The defendant in approaching the village of Wide Plains along a highway on which there were buildings and people at a rate of forty miles an hour was so endangering life. Gentlemen, there never was a simpler case as to law and fact than this one."

Lydia glanced at Wiley under her lashes. It seemed to her that O'Bannon's manner was almost perfect. She believed he had already captured the jury, but she could read nothing of Wiley's opinion in his expression. He rose more leisurely, more conversational in manner. The defense would show, he said—and his tone seemed to add "without the least difficulty"—that the motorcycle of the unfortunate young policeman had skidded and struck the automobile of the defendant, causing, to the deep chagrin of the defendant, the death of that gallant young hero. They would show that the defendant was not committing a misdemeanor at the time, for to attain a speed of twenty-five or thirty miles on a lonely road was not even violating the speed law, as everyone who owned a car knew very well. As for the indictment of manslaughter in the first degree, really—Wiley's manner seemed to say that he knew a joke was a joke, and that he had as much sense of humor as most men, but when it came to manslaughter in the first degree—"a crime, gentlemen, for which a prison sentence of twenty years may be imposed—twenty years, gentlemen." He had never in a long experience at the bar heard of a bill being found at once so spectacular and so completely at variance with the law. The defense would show them that if they followed the recommendation of his learned young friend, the district attorney, to consider the facts and the law—

His manner to O'Bannon was more paternal than patronizing. He seemed to sketch him as an eager, emotional boy intoxicated by headlines in the New York papers. Wiley radiated wisdom, pity for his client, grief for the loss of Drummond and an encouraging hope that a young man like O'Bannon would learn enough in the course of a few years to prevent his making a humiliating sort of mistake like this again. He did not say a word of this, but Lydia could see the atmosphere of his speech seeping into the jurors' minds.

Yes, she thought, it was an able opening—not the sort of ability that she would have connected with legal talent in the days when she knew less of the law; but it seemed to be the kind of magic that worked. She was pleased with her counsel, directed a flattering look at him and began to assume the air he wanted her to assume— the dovelike.

The prosecution began at once to call their witnesses—first the doctors and nurses from the hospital, establishing the cause of death. Then the exact time was established by the clock on the motorcycle—3:12, confirmed by the testimony of many witnesses. Then the ante-mortem statement was put in evidence. A long technical argument took place between the lawyers over this. It occupied all the rest of the morning session. The statement was finally admitted, but the discussion had served to impress on the jury the fact that the testimony of a witness whose credibility cannot be judged of by personal inspection, and who is saved by death from the cross-examination of the lawyer of the other side, is evidence which the law admits only under protest.

Wiley scored his first tangible success in his cross-examination of the two men who had come to Lydia's assistance. On direct examination they had testified to the high rate of speed at which Lydia had been going. Wiley, when they were turned over to him, contrived to put them in a position where they were forced either to confess that they had no knowledge of high rates of speed or else that they themselves frequently broke the law. Wiley was polite, almost kind; but he made them look foolish, and the jury enjoyed the spectacle.

This success was overshadowed by a small reverse that followed it. The prosecution had a long line of witnesses who had passed or been passed by Lydia just before the accident. One of these was a young man who was a washer in a garage about a mile away from the fatal corner. He testified in direct examination that Lydia was going forty-five miles an hour when she passed the garage.

Wiley stood up, severe and cold, his manner seeming to say, "of all things in this world, I hate a liar most!"

"And where were you at the time?"

"Standing outside the garage."

"What were you doing there?"

"Nothing."

"Nothing?"

"Smoking a pipe."

"At three o'clock in the afternoon—during working hours?" Wiley made it sound like a crime. "And during this little siesta, or holiday, you saw the defendant's car going at forty-five miles an hour—is that the idea?"

"Yes, sir."

"And will you tell the jury how it was you were able to judge so exactly of the speed of a car approaching you head-on?"

The obvious answer was that he guessed at it, but the young man did not make it.

"I do it by means of telegraph poles and counting seconds."

It then appeared that the young man was accustomed to timing automobile and motorcycle races.

Lydia saw Foster faintly smile as he glanced at his chief. Evidently the defense had fallen into a neatly laid little trap. She glanced at Wiley and saw that he was pretending to be delighted.

"Exactly, exactly!" he was saying, pointing an accusing finger at the witness; "You and Drummond used to go to motorcycle races together."

He did it very well, but it did not succeed. The jury were left with the impression that the People's witness on speed was one to be believed.

CHAPTER X

Strangely enough, the days of her trial were among the happiest and the most interesting that Lydia had ever known. They had a continuity of interest that kept her calm and equable. Usually when she woke in the softest of beds and lifted her cheek from the smoothest of pillows she asked herself what she should do that day. Choice was open to her—innumerable choices—all unsatisfactory, because her own satisfaction was the only element to be considered.

But during her trial she did not ask this question. She had an occupation and an object for living, not so much to save herself as to humiliate O'Bannon. The steady, strong interest gave shape and pattern to her days, like the thread of a string of beads.

As soon as each session was over she and Wiley, on the lawn of the courthouse or at her house if she could detain him, or she and Albee or Bobby or Miss Bennett, as the case might be, would go over each point made by the prosecution's witnesses or brought out by Wiley's cross-examination of them. The district attorney seemed to be reserving no surprises. He had a strong, straight case with Drummond's ante-mortem statement, and a great many witnesses as to Lydia's speed. The bracelet had not been admitted in evidence so far, nor had Drummond's statement referred to it, and Wiley grew more confident that it would not be allowed. The defense had felt some anxiety over the exactitude with which the hour of the accident had been established, but as Lydia did not honestly know the hour at which she had left Eleanor's nor had Eleanor or any of her servants been subpœnaed, there did not seem any danger from this point after all.

Lydia, who was to be the first witness for the defense, had thought over every point, every implication of her own testimony, until she felt sure that "that man" would not be able to catch her wrong in a single item. She did not dread the moment—she longed for it. Wiley had advised her of the danger of remembering too much—a candid "I'm afraid I don't remember that" would often convince a jury better than a too exact memory.

"And," Wiley added soothingly, "don't be frightened if the district attorney tries to browbeat you. The court will protect you, and if I seem to let it go on it will be because I see it's prejudicing the jury in your favor."

Lydia's nostrils fluttered with a long indrawn breath.

"I don't think he will frighten me," she said.

But most of all, Wiley advised her as to her bearing. She must be gentle, feminine, appealing, as if she would not voluntarily injure a fly. No matter what happened, she mustn't set her jaw and tap her foot and flash back contemptuous answers.

Lydia moved her head, looking exactly as Wiley did not want her to look.

"I cannot be appealing," she said.

"Then the district attorney will win his case," said Wiley.

There was a pause, and then Lydia said in her good-little-girl manner:

"I'll do my best."

Everybody knew that her best would be good.

The People were to close their case that morning. A witness as to Lydia's speed just before the accident was on the stand. He testified that, following her as fast as his car would go—he had no speedometer—he had not been able to keep her in sight. His name was Yakob Ussolof, and he had great difficulty with the English language. His statements were, however, clear and damaging.

The jury was almost purely Anglo-Saxon, and as Wiley rose to cross-examine the very effort he made to get the name right—"Mr.—er—Mr.—U—Ussolof"—was an appeal to their Americanism.

"Mr. Ussolof, you have driven an automobile for some years?"

"Yare, yare," said Mr. Ussolof eagerly, "for ten years now."

"How long had you owned the car you were driving on March eleventh?"

"Since fall now."

"Ah, a new car. And what was its make?"

"Flivver."

The magic word worked its accustomed miracle. Everyone smiled, and Wiley, seeing before him a jury of flivver owners, went on:

"And do you mean to tell me, Mr. Ussolof, that in the speediest car built in America you could not keep a foreign-built car going at thirty miles an hour in sight? Oh, Mr. Ussolof, you don't do us justice. We build better cars than that!"

The jury smiled, the spectators laughed, the gavel fell for order, and Mr. Wiley sat down. He had told Lydia that a jury, like an audience, loves those who make them laugh, and he sat down with an air of success. But Lydia, watching them more closely, was not so sure. As O'Bannon rose she noted the extreme gravity of his manner, his look at the jury, which seemed to say, "A man's life—a woman's liberty at stake, and you allow a mountebank to make you laugh!" It was only a look, but Lydia saw that they regained their seriousness like a lot of schoolboys when the head master enters.

"Call Alma Wooley," said O'Bannon.

90

Alma Wooley, the last witness for the People, was the girl to whom Drummond had been engaged. A little figure in the deepest mourning mounted the stand, so pale that she looked as if a strong ray would shine clear through her, and though her eyes were dry, her voice had the liquid sound that comes with much crying. Many of the jury had known her when she worked in her father's shop. She testified that her name was Alma Wooley, her age nineteen, that she lived with her father.

"Miss Wooley," said O'Bannon, "you were sent for to go to the hospital on the eleventh of this March, were you not?"

An almost inaudible "Yes, sir," was the answer.

"You saw Drummond before he died?"

She bent her head.

"How long were you with him?"

She just breathed the answer, "About an hour."

Juror Number 6 spoke up and said that he could not hear. The judge in a loud roar—offered as an example—said, "You must speak louder. You must speak so that the last juror can hear you. No, don't look at me. Look at the jury."

Thus admonished, Miss Wooley raised her faint, liquid voice and testified that she had been present while Drummond was making his statement.

"Tell the jury, what took place."

"I said—"

Her voice sank out of bearing. Wiley sprang up.

"Your Honor, I must protest. I cannot hear the witness. It is impossible for me to protect my client's interests if I cannot hear."

The stenographer was directed to read his notes aloud, and he read rapidly and without the least expression:

"Question: 'Tell the jury what took place.' Answer: 'I said, "Oh, Jack, darling, what did they do to you?" And he said, "It was her, dear. She got me after all."'"

Wiley was on his feet again, protesting in a voice that drowned all other sounds. A bitter argument between the lawyers took place. They argued with each other, they went and breathed their arguments into the ear of the judge. In the end Miss Wooley's testimony was not allowed to contain anything in reference to any previous meeting between Drummond and Lydia, but was limited to a bare confirmation of the details of Drummond's own statement. Technically the defense had won its point, but the emotional impression the girl had left was not easily effaced, nor the suspicion that the defense had something to conceal. Wiley did not cross-examine, knowing that the sooner the pathetic little figure left the stand the better. But he managed to convey that it was his sympathy with the sufferer that made him waive cross-examination.

The People's case rested.

Lydia was called. As she rose and walked behind the jury box toward the waiting Bible she realized exactly why it was that O'Bannon had put Alma on the stand the last of all his witnesses. It was to counteract with tragedy any appeal that youth and wealth and beauty might make to the emotions of the jury. Such a trick, it seemed to her, deserved a counter trick, and reconciled her to falsehood, even as she was swearing that her testimony would be the truth, the whole truth, and nothing but the truth, so help her God.

Surely it was persecution for the law to stoop to such methods. She felt as hard as steel. Women do not get fair play, she thought. Here she was, wanting to fight like a tigress, and her only chance of winning was to appear as gentle and innocuous as the dove. She testified that her name was Lydia Janetta Thorne, her age twenty-four, her residence New York.

"Miss Thorne," said Wiley, very businesslike in manner, "for how many years have you driven a car?"

"For eight years."

"As often as three or four times a week?"

"Much oftener—constantly—every day."

"Have you ever been arrested for speeding?"

"Only once—about seven years ago in New Jersey."

"Were you fined or imprisoned?"

"No, the case was dismissed."

"Have you ever, before March eleventh, had an accident in which you injured yourself or anyone else?"

"No."

"Now tell the jury as nearly as you can remember just what took place from the time you left your house on the morning of March eleventh until the accident that afternoon."

Lydia turned to the jury—not dovelike, but with a modified beam of candid friendliness that was very winning. She described her day. She had left her house about half past eleven and had run down to Miss Bellington's, a distance of thirty miles, in an hour and a half. She had expected to spend the afternoon there, but finding that her friend had an engagement she had left earlier than she expected. No, she had no motive whatsoever for getting to town quickly. On the contrary, she had extra time on her hands. No, she had not noticed the hour at which she left Miss Bellington's, but it was soon after luncheon; about twenty-five minutes before three, she should imagine.

Was she conscious of driving fast at any time?

Yes, just after leaving Miss Bellington's. There was a good piece of road and no traffic. She had run very fast—probably thirty-five miles an hour.

Did she call that fast?

Yes, she did. She achieved a very-good-little-girl manner as she said this.

For how long had she maintained this high rate of speed?

She was afraid she couldn't remember exactly, but for two or three miles. On approaching the village of Wide Plains she had slowed down to her regular rate of twenty-five miles an hour—slower as she actually entered the village. She could not say how long Drummond had been following her—she had not noticed him. She had seen him as she was entering the village—saw him reflected in her mirror. It was difficult to judge distances exactly from such a reflection. She had not been noticing him just at the moment of the accident. Yes, her decision to take the right-hand turn had been a sudden one. She had felt the impact. She believed that the policeman ran into her. She was on her own side of the road and turning to the right.

Why did she take the right-hand road, which was longer than the left?

Because it was more agreeable, and as she was in no hurry to get home she did not mind the extra distance.

After the accident she had remained and rendered every assistance in her power, going to the hospital and remaining there until the preliminary report of Drummond's condition. She had left her address and telephone number, so that the hospital could telephone her when the X-ray examination was finished.

Her friends drew a sigh of relief when her direct testimony was over. It was true, she was not an appealing figure like Alma Wooley; but she was clear, audible, direct, and her straight glance under her dark level brows was convincingly honest.

As she finished her direct testimony she looked down at her hands clasped in her lap. The important moment had come. She heard Wiley's smooth voice saying "Your witness" as if he were making the People a magnificent present. As she became aware that O'Bannon was standing up, looking at her, she raised her eyes as far as the top button of his waistcoat, and then slowly lifting both head and eyes together she stared him straight in the face.

He held her eyes for several seconds, trying, she thought, in the silence to take possession of her mind as he had taken possession of the jury's.

"Not so easy, my friend," she said to herself, and just as she said it she heard his voice saying coolly, "Look at the jury, please, not at me."

Her eyes, as she turned them in the desired direction, had a flash in them.

"Miss Thorne, at what hour did you leave Miss Bellington's?"

"I have no way of fixing it precisely—about 2:35."

"You are quite sure it was not later?"

"I cannot be sure within four or five minutes."

"What is the distance from Miss Bellington's to the scene of the accident?"

"About fifteen miles, I should think."

"Your calculation is that as the accident took place at 3:12 and you left at twenty-five minutes to three you drove fifteen miles in thirty-seven minutes—that is to say, at the rate of twenty-four miles an hour. Is that right?"

"Yes."

"And you never ran faster than thirty-five miles an hour?"

"Never."

"Don't look at me. Look at the jury, please."

She found it hard to be dovelike under this repeated admonition. "As if," she thought, "I couldn't keep my eyes off him, whereas, of course, it's human nature to look at the person who's speaking to you."

"You say," he went on, "that you had expected to stay longer at Miss Bellington's than you actually did."

"Yes."

"And what made you change your plans?"

"I found she had an engagement."

"Did she mention it on your arrival?"

"No."

"When did she mention it?"

"After luncheon."

"Was she called to the telephone during your visit?"

"No."

"Are you sure of that?"

There was a pause. The gates of Lydia's memory had suddenly opened. The telephone call, which had made no impression at the time because she had not taken in that it was from O'Bannon, suddenly came back to her. She tried hastily to see its bearing on her case, but he gave her no time.

"Answer my question, please. Will you swear there was no telephone call to your knowledge?"

"No, I cannot."

"In fact there was a telephone call?"

94

"Yes."

"It was during that telephone call that the engagement was made?"

"I cannot say—I do not know."

"How long did you stay after that telephone?"

"I left at once."

"You put on your hat?"

"Yes."

"And your veil?"

"Yes."

"And a coat?"

"Yes."

It was impossible to be dovelike under this interrogation. The jury were allowing themselves to smile.

"Had your car been left standing at the door?"

"No." She felt that her jaw was beginning to set, and she kept her foot quiet only with an effort.

"You had to wait while it was sent for?"

"Yes."

"In other words, Miss Thorne, you must have waited not less than five minutes after the telephone call came?"

"Probably not."

"Answer yes or no, please."

"No." She flung it at him.

"Then if that telephone came at thirteen minutes before three you must have left not earlier than eight minutes to three, and the accident took place at 3:12, you ran the distance—it is actually thirteen miles and a half—in twenty minutes; that is, at the rate of forty miles an hour."

Wiley protested that there was nothing in evidence to show that the telephone call had been made at thirteen minutes before three, and O'Bannon replied that with the consent of the court he would put the records of the telephone company in evidence to prove the exact hour. This point settled, a pause followed. Lydia half rose, supposing the ordeal over, but O'Bannon stopped her.

"One moment," he said. "You say you have not been arrested for exceeding the speed law for several years. Have you ever been stopped by a policeman?"

Wiley was up in protest at once.

"I object, Your Honor, on the ground of irrelevancy."

The judge said to O'Bannon, "What is the purpose of the question?"

"Credibility, Your Honor. I wish to show that the defendant is not a competent witness as to her own speed."

95

The judge locked his fingers together, with his elbows on the arms of his chair, and took a ruminative half spin.

"The fact that she was once stopped by the police will not determine that. She might have been violating some other ordinance."

"I will show, if Your Honor permits it, that it was for speeding that she was stopped."

Eventually the question was admitted; and Lydia, testifying more and more reluctantly, more and more aware that the impression she was making was bad, was forced to testify that in the autumn Drummond himself had stopped her. Asked what he had said to her, she answered scornfully that she didn't remember.

"Did he say: 'What do you think this is—a race track?'"

"I don't remember."

"Did he warn you that if you continued to drive so fast he would arrest you?"

"No."

If hate could kill, the district attorney would have been struck down by her glance.

"You don't remember any of the conversation that took place between you?"

"No."

"And you cannot explain why a traffic officer stopped you and let you go without even a warning?"

"No."

"Would it refresh your memory, Miss Thorne, to look at this bracelet which I hold in my hand?"

"I protest, Your Honor!" shouted Wiley, but a second too late. Lydia had seen the bracelet and shrunk from it—with a quick gesture of repugnance.

The line of inquiry was not permitted, the bracelet was not put in evidence, the question was ordered stricken from the records; but the total effect of her testimony was to leave in the minds of the jurors the impression that she was perfectly capable of the conduct which the prosecution attributed to her. Wiley detained her a few moments for redirect examination in the hope of regaining the dove, but in vain.

Miss Bennett was put on the stand to testify to Lydia's habitual prudence as a driver; Governor Albee testified to her excellent record; half a dozen other friends were persuasive, but could not undo the harm she had done her own case.

The district attorney put the telephone-company records in evidence, showing that only one call had been made to the Bellington house between two and three o'clock March eleventh, and that it had been made at thirteen minutes before three.

CHAPTER XI

Lydia, with the wisdom that comes specially to the courageous, knew that her trial had gone against her as she left the stand. Miss Bennett was hopeful as they drove home. Bobby actually congratulated her on the clearness and weight of what she had said.

Albee, whose own investigation had closed brilliantly the day before, came that evening to say good-by to her. He was called back to his native state on business and was leaving on a midnight train.

Since the accident Lydia had been seeing Albee every day—had used him and consulted him, and yet had almost forgotten his existence. Now as she waited for his appearance it came to her with a shock of surprise that she had once come very near to engaging herself to him; that in parting like this for a few weeks he might make the assumption that she intended to be his wife. She thought she could make her trial a good excuse for refusing to consider such a proposal. That would get rid of him without hurting his feelings. She thought of the phrase, "A woman situated as I am cannot enter into an engagement." The mere idea of such a marriage was now intensely repugnant to her. How could she have contemplated it?

He entered, leonine yet neat in his double-breasted blue serge with a pearl in his black tie. He took her hand and beamed down upon her as if many things were in his heart that he would not trouble her with at this crisis by uttering.

"Ah, my dear," he said, "I wish I might be here to-morrow to see your triumph, but I'll be back in a month or so, and then—meantime I leave you in good hands. Wiley is capital. His summing up to-morrow will be a masterpiece. And remember, if by any chance—juries are chancy, you know—they do bring in an adverse verdict, on appeal you're safe as a church." He raised a cold, rigid little hand to his lips.

With her perfect clear-sightedness she saw he was deserting her and was glad to get him out of her way. She had not even an impulse to punish him for going.

The next morning it was raining torrents. It seemed as if the globe itself were spinning in rain rather than ether. Rain beat on the streets of New York so that the asphalt ran from curb to curb in black brooks; rain swept across the open spaces of the country, and as they ran through the storm water spouted in long streams from the wheels of the car. In the court room rain ran down the windows on each side of the American flag in liquid patterns. The court room itself had a different air. The electric lights were on, the air smelled of mud and rubber coats, and Judge Homans, who suffered from rheumatism, was stiff and grim.

A blow awaited Lydia at the outset. She had not understood that the defense summed up first—that the prosecution had the last word with the jury. What might not "that man" do with the jury by means of his hypnotic sincerity? She dreaded Wiley's summing up, too, fearing it would be oratorical—all the more because he kept disclaiming any such intention.

"The day has gone by for eloquence," he kept saying. "One doesn't attempt nowadays to be a Daniel Webster or a Rufus Choate. But of course it is necessary to touch the hearts of the jury."

She thought that O'Bannon's appeal was to their heads, and yet Wiley might be right. People were such geese they might prefer Wiley's method to O'Bannon's.

As soon as court opened Wiley began his summing up, and even his client approved of his simple, leisurely manner. He was very clear and effective with the merely legal points. The crime of manslaughter in the first degree—a crime for which a sentence of twenty years might be imposed—had not been proved. Nor was there credible evidence of criminal negligence, without which a verdict of manslaughter in the second degree could not be found. As he reviewed the facts he contrived to present a picture of Lydia's youthfulness, her motherlessness, of Thorne's early beginnings as a workingman, of his death leaving Lydia an orphan. He made her beauty and wealth seem a disadvantage—a terrible temptation to an ambitious young prosecutor with an eye to newspaper headlines. He made it appear as if juries always convicted young ladies of social position, but that this particular jury by a triumph of fair-mindedness were going to be able to overcome this prejudice. One juror who had wept over Alma Wooley now shed an impartial tear for Lydia.

"Gentlemen of the jury," Wiley ended, "I ask you to consider this case on the facts and the facts alone—not to be led away by the emotional appeals of an ambitious and learned young prosecutor who has the ruthlessness that so often goes with young ambition; not to convict an innocent girl whose only crime seems to be that she is the custodian of wealth that her father, an American workingman, won from the conditions of American industry. If you consider the evidence alone you will find that no crime has been committed. I ask you, gentlemen, for a verdict of not guilty."

Lydia, with her eyes slanted down to the red carpet at a spot a few feet from O'Bannon's chair, saw that Miss Bennett turned joyfully to Eleanor, that Bobby was trying to catch her eye for a congratulatory nod; but she did not move a muscle until O'Bannon rose and crossed over to the jury. Her eyes followed him. Then she remembered to turn and give her own counsel a mechanical smile— a smile such as a nurse gives a clever child who has just built a fort on the beach which the next wave is certain to sweep away.

"Gentlemen of the jury," said O'Bannon—and he bit off his words sharply; indeed, he and Wiley seemed to have changed rôles. He who had been so cool through the trial now showed feeling, a sort of quiet passion—"this is not a personal contest between the distinguished counsel for the defense and myself. Neither my youth nor my ambition nor my alleged ruthlessness are in question. The only question is, does the evidence show beyond a reasonable doubt that the defendant committed the crime for which she has been indicted?"

Then without an extra phrase, almost without an adjective, he went on quickly piling up the evidence against her until it reached its climax in the proof of the shortness of time that had elapsed between her leaving Eleanor's and the accident.

"A particularly serious responsibility rests upon you, gentlemen, in this case. The counsel for the defense seems to assume that the rich fare less well in our courts of law than the poor. That has not been my experience. I should be glad as a believer in democracy if I could believe that justice is more available to the poor than to the rich, but I cannot. Last month in this very court a boy, younger than the defendant, who earned his living as a driver of a delivery wagon, was sentenced to three years in prison for a lesser crime, and on evidence not one-tenth as convincing as the evidence now before you. A great many of us felt sorry for that boy, too, but we felt that essential justice was done. If through sentiment or pity essential justice cannot be done in this case, if sex, wealth or conspicuous position is a guarantee of immunity, a blow will be dealt to the respect for law in this country for which you gentlemen must take the responsibility. If you find by the evidence that the defendant has committed the crime for which she is indicted I ask you to face that fact with courage and honesty, and to bring in a verdict of guilty."

There was a gentle stir in the court. The attendant announced that anyone who wished to leave the court must do so immediately. No one would be allowed to move while the judge was charging. No one moved. The doors were closed, the attendants leaning against them.

Wiley bent over and whispered, "That sort of class appeal doesn't succeed nowadays. Give yourself no concern."

Concern was the last emotion Lydia felt, or rather she felt no emotion at all. Her interest had suddenly collapsed, the game was over. She was aware that the air of the court room was close and that she felt inexpressibly tired, especially in her wrists.

The judge wheeled toward the jury and drew in his chin until it seemed to rest upon his spinal column.

"Gentlemen of the jury," he said, "we have now reached that stage in this trial when it is my duty to present the matter for your deliberation. You know that the law makes a distinction between the duty of the court and the duty of the jury. You are the judge and the only judge of the facts, but you must accept the law from the court. You must not consider whether or not you approve of the law; whether you could or could not make a better law."

Lydia suppressed a yawn.

"The tiresome old man," she thought. "He actually seems to enjoy saying all that."

His Honor went on defining a reasonable doubt:

"It is not a whim or a speculation or a surmise. It is a doubt founded on reason—on a reason which may be stated."

Lydia thought, "Imagine drawing a salary for telling people that a reasonable doubt is a doubt founded on reason." She had not imagined that she would be bored at any moment of her own trial, but she was—bored beyond belief.

"I must call your attention to Section 30 of the Penal Law, which says that whenever a crime is distinguished into degrees, the jury, if they convict, must find the degree of the crime of which the prisoner is guilty. Manslaughter is a crime distinguished into degrees—namely, the first and the second degree."

Lydia thought that if by this time the jury did not know the distinction between the two they must be half-witted, but His Honor went on to define them:

"In the first degree, when committed without design to effect death by a person committing or attempting to commit a misdemeanor."

She thought that she knew that phrase now, as when she was a child she had known some of the rules of Latin grammar—verbs conjugated with ad, ante, con, in, inter—what did they do? How funny that she couldn't remember. Her eyes had again fixed themselves on the spot on the carpet so near O'Bannon's feet that she was aware of any movement on his part, and yet she was not looking at him. A fly came limply crawling into her vision, and her eyes followed it as it lit on O'Bannon's boot. She glanced up to where his hand was resting on his knee, and then wrenched her eyes away—back to the floor again.

"If you find that the defendant is not guilty of manslaughter in the first degree you must then consider whether or not she is guilty of manslaughter in the second degree—that is, whether she occasioned the death of Drummond by an act of culpable negligence. Culpable negligence has been defined by Recorder Smyth in the case of—in the case of the People against Bedenseick as the omission to do something which a reasonable and prudent man would do, or the doing of something which such a man would not do under the circumstances of each particular case. Or, what is the same thing—"

How incredibly tiresome! She glanced at the jury. They were actually listening, drinking in the judge's words. All of a sudden she knew by his tone that he was coming to an end.

"If you find that a killing has taken place, but that it is not manslaughter in either degree, then it is your duty to acquit. If on the other hand you find the defendant guilty in either degree you must not consider the penalty which may be imposed. That is the province of the court; yours is to consider the facts. Such, gentlemen, is the law. The evidence is before you. You are at liberty to believe or to disbelieve the testimony of any witness in part or as a whole, according to your common sense. Weigh the testimony, giving each fact its due proportion; and then, according to your best judgment, render your verdict."

His Honor was silent. There were a few requests to charge from both sides, and the jury filed solemnly out. Almost without a pause the next case was called, the attendant's voice ringing out as before—"The case of the People against—"

Lydia felt disinclined to move, as if even her bones were made of some soft dissoluble material. Then she saw that she had no choice. The next prisoner was waiting for her place—an unshaven, hollow-eyed Italian, with a stout, gray-clad lawyer who looked like Caruso at his side. As she left the court she could hear the clerk calling the new jury.

"William Roberts."

"Seat Number One."

Judge Homans flattered himself particularly on the celerity with which his court moved.

CHAPTER XII

Several of the New York papers the next morning carried editorials commending the verdict. Lydia sitting up in bed with a breakfast tray on her knee, read them coolly through.

"The safety of the highways"—"the irresponsibility of the younger generation, particularly among those of great wealth"—"pity must not degenerate into sentimentality"—"the equal administration of our laws—"

So the public was pleased with the verdict, was it? It little knew. She herself was filled with bitterness. The moment of the delivery of the verdict had been terrible to her.

She had not minded the hours of waiting. She had felt deadened, without special interest in what the jury decided. But this had changed the moment word came that the jury had reached a verdict. There was a terrible interval while the familiar roll of their names was called for the last time. Then she was told to stand up and face them, or rather to face the foreman, Josiah Howell, a bearded man with a lined brown face. He looked almost tremulously grave.

Lydia set her jaw, looking at him and thinking, "What business have you interfering in my fate?" But he was not the figure she was most aware of. It was the district attorney, whose excitement she knew was as great as her own.

"How say you?" said a voice. "Guilty or not guilty?"

"Guilty of manslaughter in the second degree," answered the foreman.

Lydia knew every eye in the court room was turned on her. She had heard of defendants who fainted on hearing an adverse verdict—keeled over like dead people. But one does not faint from anger, and anger was Lydia's emotion—anger that "that man" had actually obtained the verdict he wanted. Her breath came fast and her nostrils dilated. How sickening that she had nothing to do but stand there and let him triumph! No subsequent reversal would take away this moment from him.

The jury was thanked and dismissed. Wiley was busy putting in pleas that would enable her to remain at liberty during the appeal of her case. She stood alone, still now as a statue. She was thinking that some day the world should know by what methods that verdict had been obtained.

She had behaved well during her trial; had lived a life of retirement, seeing no one but Wiley and her immediate friends. But there was no further reason for playing a part. On the contrary she felt it would relieve her spirit to show the world—and O'Bannon—that she was not beaten yet. She did not intend to look upon herself as a criminal because he had induced a jury to convict her.

She bought herself some new clothes and went out every night, dancing till dawn and sleeping till noon. She began a new flirtation, this time with a good-looking insolent young English actor, Ludovic Blythe, hardly twenty-one, with a strange combination of wickedness and naïveté that some English boys possess. Her friends disapproved of him heartily.

At his suggestion she engaged a passage for England for early July. Wiley warned her that it was unlikely that the decision in her case would be handed down as soon as that, and if it were not she could not leave the country.

"There's no harm in engaging a cabin, is there?" she answered.

Her plan was to take in the end of the London season, with a few house parties in the English country, to spend September in Venice, two weeks in Paris buying clothes, and to come home in October.

"To Long Island?" Miss Bennett asked.

"Of course. Where else?" answered Lydia. "Do you think I shall allow myself to be driven out of my own home?"

But July came without the decision, and Lydia was obliged to cancel her passage. She was annoyed.

"Those lazy old judges," she said, "have actually adjourned for two months, and now I can't get off until September." Her tone indicated that she was doing a good deal for the law of her country, changing her plans like this.

O'Bannon, she heard, was taking a holiday too—going to Wyoming for a month. She thought that she would like to see something of the West, but instead she took a house at Newport for August—a fevered month. Blythe came to spend Sunday with her and stayed two weeks, fell in love with May Swayne, attempted to use his position as a guest of Lydia's to make himself appear a more desirable suitor in the eyes of the Swayne family—a solid old-fashioned fortune—and was turned out by Lydia after a scene of unusual violence.

A feud followed in which many people took—and changed—sides. Lydia fought gayly, briskly in the open. Her object was not Blythe's death, but his social extinction, and her method was not cold steel but ridicule. The war was won when May was made to see him as an impossible figure, comic, on the make—as perhaps he was, but no more so than when Lydia herself had received him.

After this, though he lingered on a few days at a hotel, his ultimate disappearance was certain. Lydia and May remained friends throughout—as much friends as they had ever been. Since the day of their first meeting the two women had never permitted any man to be a friend of both of them.

Albee came and spent a brief twenty-four hours with her between a midnight train and Sunday boat. He was in the midst of a campaign as United States senator from his own state—certain of election. Lydia was kind and patient with him, but frankly bored.

"There's more stuff in Bobby," she confided to Benny, "who doesn't expect you to tremble at his nod. I hate fake strong men. I always feel tempted to call their bluff. It's a hard rôle they want to play. If they don't break you, you despise them. If they do—why, you're broken, no good to anyone."

She asked Eleanor to come and spend August with her, but Eleanor refused, saying, what was true enough, that she couldn't bear Newport. She could bear even less constant association with Lydia at this moment. Lydia's one preoccupation when they were together was to destroy Eleanor's friendship for O'Bannon. Often in old times Eleanor had laughed at the steady persistence that Lydia put into this sort of campaign of hate, but she could not laugh now, for as a matter of fact her friendship with O'Bannon was already destroyed. She hardly saw him, and if she did there was a veil between them. He was kind, he was open with her, he was everything except interested.

Eleanor loved O'Bannon, but with so intellectual a process that she was not far wrong in considering it was a friendship. She would have married him if he had asked her, but she would have done so principally to insure herself of his company. If anyone could have guaranteed that they would continue all their lives to live within a few yards of each other she would have been content—content even with the knowledge that every now and then some other less reasonable woman would come and sweep him away from her. She knew he was of a temperament susceptible to terrible gusts of emotion, but she considered that that was her hold upon him—she was so safe.

The remoteness that came to their relation now indicated another woman, and yet she knew his everyday life well enough to know that he was seeing no one except herself and Alma Wooley; and though there was some gossip about his attention to the girl, Eleanor felt she understood the reason for it. Alma made him feel emotionally what he knew rationally—that his prosecution of Lydia had been merely an act of justice. Alma thought him the greatest of men and was tremulously grateful to him for establishing her dead

104

lover as a hero—a man killed in the performance of his duty. To her imagination Lydia was an unbelievable horror, like a wicked princess in a fairy tale. Eleanor wondered if she did not seem somewhat the same to O'Bannon. He never mentioned her name when she, Eleanor, spoke of her. It was like dropping a stone into a bottomless well. She listened and listened, and nothing came back from O'Bannon's abysmal silence. He spoke of her only once, and that was when he came to say good-by to Eleanor the day he started for Wyoming. He was eager to get away—into those mountains, to sleep under the stars and forget everything and everybody in the East.

"Mercy," Eleanor thought, "how ruthless men are! I wouldn't let any friend of mine see I was glad to leave him, even if I were."

"It's a rotten job—mine," he said. "I'm always sending people to prison who are either so abnormal they don't seem human or else so human they seem just like myself."

Presently Eleanor mentioned that Lydia had asked her to go to Newport for a month. O'Bannon turned on her sharply.

"And are you going?"

She said no, but it did not save her from his contempt.

"I don't see how you can be a friend of that woman's, Eleanor," he said.

"Lydia has the most attaching qualities when you know her, Dan."

"Attaching!" he broke out with a suppressed irritation she had never seen—a strange hate of her, Eleanor, for saying such a thing. "Arrogant, inflexible, using all her gifts—her brains and her incredible beauty—just to advance her own selfish ends!"

An impulse based partly on pure loyalty but partly on the idea that she could improve her position by showing her friend was not quite a monster made her answer, "You wouldn't believe, Dan, how if she really cares for you she can be tender almost clinging."

"For God's sake don't let's talk of her!" said O'Bannon, and it was on this note that they parted.

He wrote to her only once, though his letters to his mother were always at her disposal. She saw a great deal of the old lady, who developed a mild pleurisy as soon as her son's back was turned and didn't want Dan told of it. Eleanor spent most of that hot August taking care of her.

"I want him to have an uninterrupted holiday," said Mrs. O'Bannon firmly. "He hasn't been well. He doesn't sleep as he ought to, and he's cross, and you know it's not like Dan to be cross."

On the last day of August he was back, lean and sunburned,

announcing himself to be in excellent condition. His first question was about the Thorne case.

"Are you anxious about it?" said his mother.

"Not a bit. They can't reverse us," he answered.

After Labor Day Lydia moved back to her Long Island house, and she was there when the decision in her case was handed down. The verdict of the lower court was sustained. It was a great blow to her—perhaps the first real blow she had ever received. She had so firmly made up her mind that the former verdict had been the result of undue influence of the district attorney that she had thought it impossible that the higher court would uphold it. Another triumph for "that man!" The idea of punishment was horrible to her—to be fined as a criminal. She still did not conceive it a possibility that she could be sent to prison.

"I can think of lots of ways in which I'd rather spend a thousand dollars," was her only comment.

But day and night she thought of the scene in court when she must present herself for sentence. In secret her courage failed her. It would be the visible symbol of O'Bannon's triumph over her. Yet her will threw itself in vain against the necessity. Nothing but death could save her. It would be short anyhow. She knew how it would be. She and Wiley would appear in the midst of some other wretch's trial. There would be whisperings about the judge's desk, and O'Bannon would be there—not looking at her, but triumphing in his black heart, and the judge would say "A thousand-dollar fine," or—no, nothing so succinct. He would find it an opportunity to talk about her and her case first. And then she would pay the money and leave court, a convicted criminal.

And then the second stage would begin. It would be her turn. She would give her life to getting even with O'Bannon. She who had always needed a purpose—a string on which to thread her life—had found it in hate. Most people found it in love, but for her part she enjoyed hate. It was exciting and active, and, oh, what a climax it promised! Yes, like the adventuress in the melodrama, she would go to him herself and say: "I've waited ten years to ruin you, and now I've done it. Have you been wondering all these years what was against you—what held you back and poisoned everything you touched? It was I!"

Other people, she knew, thought such things and never put them in action. But she had no reason to distrust the power of her own will, and never had she willed anything as she willed this. She began to arrange it. There were three ways in which you could hurt a man—through his love, through his ambitions and through his finances. A crooked politician like O'Bannon might suffer most by

106

being ruined politically. She must always keep some hold on Albee for that. Money probably wouldn't greatly matter to O'Bannon. But love—he was an emotional creature. Women, she felt sure, played a tremendous rôle in his life. And he was attractive to them—accustomed to success probably. Oh, to think that she had been for a few seconds acquiescent in his arms! And yet that meant that she had power over him. She knew she had power. Should that be her method—to make him think that she had seen him not as an enemy but as a hero, a crusader, a master, that she was an adoring victim? Oh, how easily she could make love to him, and how successfully! She could imagine going down on her knees to him, winding herself about him, only she must have the climax ready so that at the same second she would destroy both his love and career. She must wait, and it would be hard to wait; but she must wait until she and Albee had dug a deep pit. Then she would call him to her and he would have to come. It was by thinking these thoughts that she managed to come into court calm and cold as steel.

"What have you now to say why the judgment of the court should not be pronounced upon you?"

The judge beckoned her and Wiley to his desk. O'Bannon was already there, standing so close that her arm would have touched his if she had not shrunk away. She trembled with hate. It was horrible to be so near him. She heard his own breath unsteadily drawn. Across the space that parted them waves of some tangible emotion leaped to and fro. She looked up at him and found that he, with clenched hands and drawn brows, was looking at her. So they remained.

"Your Honor," said Wiley in his smooth tones, "I would like to ask that a fine rather than a prison sentence be imposed on this prisoner, not only on account of her youth and previous good record, but because to a woman of her sheltered upbringing a prison sentence is a more severe punishment than the law contemplated."

"I entirely disagree with you, counselor," said the judge in a loud ringing tone. "The feature that makes the court so reluctant ordinarily to impose prison sentences is the subsequent difficulty in earning a living. That consideration is entirely absent in the present case. On the other hand, to impose a fine would be palpably ridiculous, constituting for this defendant no punishment whatsoever. I sentence this prisoner"—the judge paused and drew in his chin—"to not less than three nor more than seven years in state's prison."

She heard Wiley passionately pleading with Judge Homans. A blue-coated figure was now standing beside her. It was still incredible.

"This is your doing," she heard her own voice saying very softly to O'Bannon.

To her surprise she saw that emotion, what emotion she did not know, made it impossible for him to answer. His eyes stared at her out of a face whiter than her own. It was his emotion that communicated her own situation to her. His hand on the desk was shaking. She knew he could not have done what she proceeded to do. She turned and walked with the policeman to the iron-latticed passageway that led to jail.

As the door clanged behind her O'Bannon turned and walked out of court, and getting into his car drove away westward. At two in the morning Eleanor was waked by a telephone from Mrs. O'Bannon. Dan had not come home. She was afraid something had happened to him. A man in his position had many enemies. Did Eleanor think that some friend or lover of that Thorne girl—

Oh, no, Eleanor was sure not!

The next morning—for a small town holds few secrets—she knew that O'Bannon had returned at six o'clock, drunk.

"Oh, dear heaven," thought Eleanor, "must he re-travel that road?"

CHAPTER XIII

Lydia and her guard arrived at the prison early in the evening. She had been travelling all through the hot, bright September day. For the first hour she had been only aware of the proximity of the guard, of the crowded car, the mingled smell of oranges and coal smoke, the newspaper on the floor, trodden by every foot, containing probably an account of her departure for her long imprisonment. Then, her eyes wandering to the river, she suddenly remembered that it would be years before she saw mountains and flowing water again. Perhaps she would never see them again.

During the previous winter she had gone with Benny and Mrs. Galton to visit a prison in a neighboring state—a man's prison. It was considered an unfortunate example. Scenes from that visit came back to her in a series of pictures. A giant negro highwayman weaving at an immense loom with a heavy, hopeless regularity. Black, airless punishment cells—"never used nowadays," the warden had said lightly, and had been corrected by a low murmur from the keeper; two of them were in use at the moment. The tiers of ordinary cells, not so very much better, with their barred loopholes. And the smells—the terrible prison smells. At their best, disinfectant and stale soap; at worst—Lydia never knew that it was possible to remember a smell as she now remembered that one. But most of all she remembered the chalky pallor of some of the prisoners, some obviously tubercular, others twitching with nervous affections. She doubted coolly if many people were strong enough to go through years of that sort of thing.

So she would look at the river as if she might never see it again.

They were already in the Highlands, and the hills on the eastern side—her side of the river—were throwing a morning shadow on the water, while across the way the white marble buildings at West Point shone in the sunlight. Storm King with its abrupt bulk interposed itself between the two sections of new road—the road which Lydia had so much desired to see finished. She and Bobby had had a plan to motor along it to the Emmonses some day—Newburgh. There was a hotel there where she had stopped once for luncheon on her way to Tuxedo from somewhere or other. Then presently the bridge at Poughkeepsie, and then the station at which she had got out when she had spent Sunday with the Emmonses, the day Evans had been arrested and had confessed to that man—There was the very pillar she had waited beside while the chauffeur looked up her bags. Now the river began to narrow, there were marshy islands in it, and huge shaky ice houses along the brink. It all unrolled before her like a picture that she was never going to see again. Then Albany, set on its hills, and the train, turning sharply, rumbled over the bridge into the blackened station. Almost everybody in the car got out here, for the train stopped some time; but she and her guard remained sitting silently side by side. Then presently they were going on again, through the beautiful wide fertile valley of the Mohawk—They were getting near, very near. She felt not frightened but physically sick. She wondered if her hair would be cut short. Of course it would. It seemed to her like an indignity committed by O'Bannon's own hand.

It was dark when they reached the station, so dark that she could not get a definite idea of anything but the great wall of the prison, and the clang of the unbarring of the great gate. Later she came to know the doorway with its incongruous beauty—the white door with its fanlight and side windows, and two low stairways curving up to it, and, above, the ironwork porch, supported on square ironwork columns of a leaf pattern, suggestive somehow of an old wistaria vine. But now she knew nothing between the gate and the opening of the front door.

She entered what might have been the wide hall of an old-fashioned and extraordinarily bare country house. A wide stairway rose straight before her, and wide, old-fashioned doors opened formally to left and right.

She was taken into the room at the right—the matron's room. While her name and age and crime were being registered she stood staring straight before her where bookshelves ran to the ceiling. She could recognise familiar bindings—the works of Marion Crawford and Mrs. Humphry Ward.

Calm brown-eyed women seemed to surround her, but she would not even look at them. Their impersonal kindness seemed to be founded on the insulting knowledge of her utter helplessness. They chatted a little with the guard who had brought her. Was the train late? Well, not as bad as last time.

She wondered how soon they would cut her hair.

After a little while she was taken through a long corridor directly to a spacious bathroom. Her clothes, wrapped in a sheet, were borne away. At this Lydia gave a short laugh. It pleased her as a sign that the routine in her case was palpably ridiculous—to take away her things as if they were infected. She was given a bath, a nightgown of most unfriendly texture was handed to her, and presently she was locked in her cell—still in possession of her hair.

She felt like an animal in a trap—could imagine herself

110

running along the floor smelling at cracks for some hope of escape, with that strange head motion, up and down, up and down, of a newly caged animal.

More even than the locks and bolts, she minded the open grille in the door, like an eye through which she might at any moment of the day or night be spied upon. At every footstep she prepared herself to meet with a defiant stare the eyes of an inspector. The cell was hardly a cell, but a room larger than most hall bedrooms. The bed had a white cover; so had the table; and the window, though barred, was large. But this made no impression on Lydia. She was conscious of being locked in. Only her pride and her hard common sense kept her from beating at the door with her bare hands and making one of those screaming outbreaks so familiar to prison officials.

She who had never been coerced was now to be coerced in every action, surrounded everywhere by symbols of coercion. She who had been so intense an individualist that she had discarded a French model if she saw other women wearing it was now to wear a striped gingham dress of universal pattern. She whose competent white hands had never done a piece of useful work was sentenced to not less than three or more than seven years of hard labor. What would that be—hard labor? The vision of that giant negro working hopelessly at his loom was before her all night long.

All night long she wandered up and down her cell, now and then laying her hand on the door to assure herself of the incredible fact that it was locked. Only for a few minutes at dawn she fell asleep, forgetting the catastrophe, the malignant fate that had overtaken her, and woke imagining herself at home.

When her cell door was unlocked she stepped out into the same corridor along which she had passed the night before. She found it a blaze of sunlight. Great patches of sunlight fell in barred patterns on the boards of the floor, scrubbed as white as the deck of a man-of-war. Remembering the gloomy granite loopholes of her imagination, this sun seemed insolently bright.

The law compels every prisoner, unless specially exempted, to spend an hour a day in school. Lydia's examination was satisfactory enough to exempt her, but she was set to work in the schoolroom, giving out books, helping with papers, erasing the blackboards, collecting the chalk and erasers. In this way the whole population of the prison—about seventy-five women—passed before her in the different grades. She might have found interest and opportunity, but she was in no humor to be coöperative.

She sat there despising them all, feeling her own essential difference—from the bright-eyed Italian girl who had known no

111

English eighteen months before and was now so industrious a student, to the large, calm, unbelievably good-tempered teacher. The atmosphere of the room was not that of a prison school but of a kindergarten. That was what annoyed Lydia—that these women seemed to like to learn. They spelled with enthusiasm—these grown women. Up and down pages they went, spelling "passenger" and "transfer" and "station"—it was evidently a lesson about a trolley car. Was she, Lydia Thorne, expected to join joyfully in some such child-like discipline? In mental arithmetic the competition grew keener. Muriel, a soft-voiced colored girl, made eight and seven amount to thirteen. The class laughed gayly. Lydia covered her face with her hands.

"Oh," she thought, "he might better have killed me than this!"

It seemed to her that this terrible impersonal routine was turning on her like a great wheel and grinding her into the earth. What incredible perversity it Was that no one—no prisoner, no guard, not even the clear-eyed matron—would see the obvious fact that she was not a criminal as these others were.

Had O'Bannon's power reached even into the isolation of prison and dictated that she should be treated like everyone else— she who was so different from these uneducated, emotional, unstable beings about her?

It was her former maid, Evans, who destroyed this illusion. The different wards of the prison ate separately; and as Evans was not in her ward they did not meet during the day. They met in the hour after tea, before the prisoners were locked in their cells for the night; an hour when in the large hall they were allowed to read and talk and sew and tat—tatting was very popular just then.

Lydia had sunk into a rocking-chair. She could not fix her mind on a book, and she did not know how to sew or tat, and talk for talk's sake had never been one of her amusements. She was thinking "One day has gone by out of perhaps seven years. In seven years I shall be thirty-three," when she felt some one approaching her, and looking up she saw it was Evans.

Evans, in a striped cotton, did not look so different from the lady's maid of the old days, except, as Lydia noticed with vague surprise, she had put on weight. She came with the hurried walk that made her skirts flip out at her heels—the same walk with which she used to come when she was late to dress Lydia for dinner. She almost expected to hear the familiar, "What will you wear, miss?" A dozen memories flashed into her mind—Evans polishing her jewels in the sunlight, Evans locked in the disordered bedroom refusing her confidence to everyone, and then collapsing and confessing to "that man."

112

She looked away from the approaching figure, hoping the girl would take the hint; but no, Evans was drawing up a chair with something of the manner of a hostess to a new arrival.

"Oh, Evans!" was Lydia's greeting, very much in her old manner.

"You'd better call me Louisa here—I mean, it's first names we use," said Evans.

The fact had already been called to her former employer's attention by Muriel, who had done nothing but call her Lydia in a futile effort to be friendly. She steeled herself to hear it from Evans, who, however, managed to avoid it. She gossiped of the prison news, and tried to cheer and help this newcomer with whatever wisdom she had acquired. Lydia neither moved nor answered nor again looked up.

"As the matron says," Evans ran on, "the worst is over when you get here. It's the trial and the sentence and the journey that's worst. After a week or so you'll begin to get used to it."

Lydia's nostrils trembled.

"I shall never get used to it," she said. "I don't belong here. What I did was no crime."

There was a short pause. Lydia waited for Evans' cordial agreement to what seemed a self-evident assertion. None came. Instead she said gently, as she might have explained to a child, "Oh, miss, they all think that!"

"Think what?"

"That what they did was no real harm—that they were unjustly condemned. There isn't one here who won't tell you that. The worse they are the more they think it."

Lydia had looked up from her contemplation of the gray rag rug. No sermon could have stopped her as short as that—the idea that she was exactly like all the other inmates. She protested, more to herself than to Evans.

"But it is different! What I did was an accident, not a deliberate crime."

Evans smiled her old, rare, gentle smile.

"But the law says it was a crime."

Horrible! Horrible but true! Lydia was to find that every woman there felt exactly as she did; that she was a special case; that she had done nothing wrong; that her conviction had been brought about by an incompetent lawyer, a vindictive district attorney, a bribed jury, a perjured witness. The first thing each of them wanted to explain was that she—like Lydia—was a special case.

The innocent-looking little girl who had committed bigamy. "Isn't it to laugh?" said she. "Gee, when you think what men do to us! And I get five years for not knowing he was dead! And what harm did I do him anyway?"

And the gaunt elderly stenographer who had run an illicit mail-order business for her employers. One of them had evidently occupied her whole horizon, taking the place of all law, moral and judicial.

"He said it was positively legal," she kept repeating, believing evidently that the judge and jury had been pitifully misinformed.

And there was the stout middle-aged woman with sandy hair and a bland competent manner—she was competent. She had made a specialty of real-estate frauds.

"I was entirely within the law," she said, as one hardly interested to argue the matter.

And there were gay young mulatto girls and bright-eyed Italians, who all said the same thing—"everyone does it; only the other girl squealed on me"—and there were the egotists, who were never going to get into this mess again. Some girls had to steal for a living; they had brains enough to go straight. Even the woman who had attempted to kill her husband felt she had been absolutely within her rights and after hearing her story Lydia was inclined to agree with her.

Only Evans seemed to feel that her sentence had been just.

"No, it wasn't right what I did," she said, and she stood out like a star, superior to her surroundings. She only was learning and growing in the terrible routine. It soon began to seem to Lydia that this little fool of a maid of hers was a great person. Why?

Locked in her cell from dark to daylight, Lydia spent much of the time in thinking. Like a great many people in this world, she had never thought before. She had particularly arranged her life so she should not think. Most people who think they think really dream. Lydia was no dreamer. She lacked the romantic imagination that makes dreams magical. Clear-sighted and pessimistic when she looked at life, the reality had seemed hideous, and she looked away as quickly as possible, looked back to the material beauty with which she had surrounded herself and the pleasant activities always within reach. Now, cut off from pleasure and beauty, it seemed to her for the first time as if there were a real adventure in having the courage to examine the whole scheme of life. Its pattern could hardly be more hideous than that of every day.

What was she? What reason had she for living? What use could life be put to? What was the truth?

A verse she could not place kept running through her head:

Quand j'ai connu la Vérité,
J'ai cru que c'était une amie;
Quand je l'ai comprise et sentie,
J'en étais déjà dégoûté.

Et pourtant elle est éternelle,
Et ceux qui se sont passés d'elle
Ici-bas ont tout ignoré.

She had been deliberately ignorant of much of life—of everything.

She went through a period of despair, all the worse because, like a face in a nightmare, it was featureless. It was despair, not over the fact that she was in prison but over the whole scheme of the universe, the futile hordes of human beings living and hoping and failing and passing away.

Despair paralyzed her bodily activities. Her mind, even her giant will, failed her. She could neither sleep nor eat, and after a week of it was taken to the hospital. The rumor ran through the prison that she was going mad—that was the way it always began. She lay in the hospital two days, hardly moving. Her face seemed to have shrunk and her eyes to have grown large and fiery. The doctor came and talked to her. She would not answer him; she would not meet his gaze; she would do nothing but draw long unnatural breaths like sighs.

In the room next to her there was a mother with a six-months-old baby. Lydia at the best of times had never been much interested in babies, though all young animals made a certain appeal to her. Her friends' babies, swaddled and guarded by nurses, lacked the spontaneous charm of a kitten or a puppy. This baby, however—Joseph his name was, and he was always so referred to—was different. He spent a great deal of time alone, sitting erect in his white iron crib. In spite of the conditions of his birth, he was calm, pink-cheeked and healthy. The first day that Lydia was up she glanced at him as she passed the door. He gave her somehow the impression of leading a life apart. At first she only used to stare at him from the doorway; then she ventured in, leaned on the crib, offered him a finger to which he clung, invented a game of clapping of hands, and was rewarded by a toothless smile and a long complicated gurgle of delight.

The sound was too much for Lydia—the idea that the baby was glad to be starting out on the tortured adventure of living. She went back to her own room in tears, weeping not for her own griefs but because all human beings were so infinitely pathetic.

115

The next day, Anna, the mother, came in while she was bending over the crib. Lydia knew her story, the common one—the story of a respectable, sheltered girl falling suddenly, wildly in love with a handsome boy, and finding, when after a few months he wearied of her, that she had never been his wife—that he was already married.

Lydia looked at the neat, blond, spectacled woman beside her. It was hard to imagine her murdering anyone. She seemed gentle, vague, perhaps a little defective. Later in their acquaintance she told Lydia how she had done it. She had not minded his perfidy so much, until he told her that she had known all along they weren't married—that she'd done it with her eyes open—that she had been "out for a good time." He was a paperhanger among other things, and a great pair of shears had been lying on the table. The first thing she knew they were buried in his side.

Lydia could not resist asking her whether she regretted what she had done.

The girl considered. "I think it was right for him to die," she said, but she was sorry about Joseph. In a little while the baby would be taken from her and put into a state institution. She was maternal—primitively maternal—and her real punishment was not imprisonment but separation from her child. Lydia saw this without entirely understanding it.

The girl had said to her: "I suppose you can't imagine killing anyone?"

Lydia assured her that she could—oh, very easily. She went back to her room thinking that she was more a murderess at heart than this girl, who was now nothing but a mother.

When she came out of the hospital she was not put back at the schoolroom work but was sent to the kitchen. This was an immense tiled room which gave the impression to those who first entered it of being entirely empty. Then the eye fell on a row of copper containers—three of them as tall as she—one for tea, one for coffee, one for hot water, and three smaller pots, round like witches' caldrons, for the cooking of cereals and meats and potatoes. The baking was done in an adjacent alcove. There Lydia was put to work. Gradually the process began to interest her—the mixing of the dough and the baking of dozens of loaves at a time in a great oven with rotating shelves in it. The oven, like all ovens, had its caprices, dependent upon the amount of heat being used by the rest of the institution. Lydia set herself to master the subject. A certain strain of practical competence in her had never before had its expression.

116

As Lydia began to emerge from her depression she clung to Evans, who had first made her see that she could not think anything human alien to herself. The disciplined little Englishwoman, sincere and without self-pity, seemed the purveyor of wisdom. She saw her own mistakes clearly. William—William was the pale young footman, about whom they talked a good deal—had urged her for a long time to pick up a ten-dollar bill now and then or a forgotten bit of jewelry. She had never felt any temptation to do so until Lydia had been so indifferent about the loss of the bracelet. What was the use of caring so much about the safety of the jewels if the owner cared so little?

"Oh, that bracelet!" murmured Lydia, remembering how she had last seen it in O'Bannon's hand in court. For a moment she did not follow what Evans was saying, and came back in the midst of a sentence.

"—and made me see that because you were wrong that did not make me right. Then I got ready to confess. He made me see that the real harm was done and over when I took a thing that wasn't mine, and that the only way to get back was to obey the law and go to prison and get through with it as quick as I could. I owe a lot to him, Lydia—not that he preached at me, but his eyes looked right into me."

"Of whom are you speaking?" Lydia asked sharply.

"Of Mr. O'Bannon," answered Evans, and a reverent tone came into her voice.

This was too much for Lydia. She broke out, assuring Evans that she had been quite right to take the jewels. She, Lydia, now knew what a thoughtless, inconsiderate employer she had always been. But as for "that man," Evans must see that he had only tricked her into confessing in order to save himself trouble. It was a feather in his cap—to get a confession. He had not thought about saving her soul. Lydia stamped her foot in the old way but without creating any impression on the bewitched girl, who insisted on being grateful to the man who had imprisoned her.

"Is that what he is looking for from me?" thought Lydia.

Long, long winter nights in prison are excellent periods for thinking out a revenge. She saw it would not be easy to revenge herself on O'Bannon. If it were Albee it would be simple enough—she would make him publicly ridiculous. To wound that sensitive egotism would be to slay the inner man. If it were Bobby—poor dear

Bobby—she would destroy his self-confidence and starve him to death through his own belief that he was worthless. But what could she do to O'Bannon but kill him—or make him love her? Perhaps threaten to kill him. She tried to think of him on his knees, pleading for his life. But no, she couldn't give the vision reality. He wouldn't go down on his knees; he wouldn't plead; he'd stand up to her in defiance and she would be forced to shoot to prove that she had meant what she said.

She had been in prison about three months when one morning word came to the kitchen that she was wanted in the reception room. This meant a visitor. It was not Miss Bennett's day. It must be a specially privileged visitor. Her guest was Albee.

Prisoners whose conduct was good enough to keep them in the first grade were allowed to see visitors once a week. Miss Bennett came regularly, and Eleanor had come more than once. Lydia was very eager to see these two, but was not eager to see anyone else. There was always a terrible moment of shyness with newcomers—an awkward ugly moment. She did not wish to see anyone who did not love her in a simple human way that swept away restraint.

She did not want to see Albee, and she was equally sure he did not want to see her but had been driven by the politician's fear of leaving behind him in his course onward and upward any smoldering fires of hatred which a little easy kindness might quench. As a matter of fact, she did not hate Albee—nor like him. She simply recognized him as a useful person whom all her life she would go on using. This coming interview must serve to attach him to her, so that if in the future she needed a powerful politician to help her destroy O'Bannon she would have one ready to her hand. She knew exactly and instinctively how to manage Albee—not by being appealing and friendly. If she were nice to him he would go away feeling that that chapter in his life was satisfactorily closed. But if she were hostile, if she made him uncomfortable, he would work to win back her friendship. Prisoner as she was, she would be his master. She arranged herself, expression and spirit alike, to meet him sternly.

She did not stop to consider the impression she might make on her visitor—in her striped dress and her prison shoes. It was never Lydia's habit to think first of the impression she was making.

She was brought to the matron's room, and then crossing the hall she entered the bare reception room, with its chill, white mantelpiece, the fireplace blocked by a sheet of metal, its empty center table and stiff straight-backed chairs. She entered without any anticipation of what was in store for her, and saw a tall figure just turning from the window. It was O'Bannon. She had just a blurred vision of his gray eyes and the hollows in his cheeks. Then her wrists and knees seemed to melt, her heart turned over within her; everything grew yellow, green and black, and she fainted—falling gently full length at the feet of the district attorney.

When she came to she was in her own cell. She turned her head slowly to right and left.

"Where is that man?" she said. She was told he had gone.

Of course he had gone—gone without waiting for her recovery, without speaking to anyone else. There was the proof that he was vindictive; that he had come to humiliate her, to feast his eyes on her distress. He had hardly dared hope that she would faint at his feet. There was real cruelty for you, she thought—to ruin a woman's life and then to come and enjoy the spectacle. What a story for him to go home with, to remember and smile over, to tell, perhaps, to his mother or Eleanor!

"The poor girl!" he might say with tones of false pity in his voice. "At the mere sight of me she fainted dead away and lay at my feet in her prison dress, her hands coarsened by hard work—"

This last proof of her utter defenselessness infuriated her. She was justified in her revenge, whatever it might be. The thought of it ran through all her dreams like a secret romance.

It began to take shape in her mind as political ruin. She knew from Eleanor that he had ambitions. He had taken the district attorneyship with the intention of making it lead to higher political office. She had fancies of defeating him in a campaign, using all the tragedy of her own experience to rouse the emotions of audiences. Easier to destroy him within his own party by Albee's help—easier, but not so spectacular. He might not know who had done it unless she went to him and explained. Over that interview her mind often lingered.

As her ideas of retribution took shape she became happier in her daily life, as if the thought of O'Bannon sucked up all the poison in her nature and left her other relations sweeter.

If Lydia had but known it, her revenge was complete when she fell at his feet. The months she had spent in prison had been paradise compared to the months he had spent at large. The verdict in the case had hardly been rendered before he had begun to be tortured by doubts as to his own motives. It was no help to him that his reason offered him a perfect defense. The girl was a criminal—reckless, irresponsible and untruthful, more deserving of punishment than most of the defendants who came into court. If there were any personal animus in his prosecution there was an excuse for it in the fact that Albee had certainly come to him with

119

the intention of exerting dishonorable pressure in her behalf. Everyone he saw—his mother, Eleanor, Foster, Judge Homan—all believed that he had followed the path of duty in spite of many shining temptations to be weakly pitiful. But he himself knew—and gradually came to admit—that he had done what he passionately desired to do. Even he could not look deeply enough into his own heart to understand his motives, but he began to be aware of a secret growing remorse poisoning his inner life.

The thought of her in prison was never out of his mind, and it was a nightmare prison he thought of. In the first warm September days he imagined the leaden, airless heat of cells. When October turned suddenly cold and windy he remembered how she was accustomed to playing golf on the windy links and how he had once seen her driving from a tee near the roadside with her skirts wrapped about her by her vigorous swing. He gave up playing bridge—the memories were too poignant. And after Eleanor had once mentioned that Lydia was fond of dancing he could not listen to a strain of dance music. Christmas was a particularly trying time to him, with all its assumption of rejoicing—a prison Christmas!

During the holidays he was in New York for a few days. His theory was that lack of exercise was the reason for his not sleeping better. He used to take long walks in the afternoon and evening so as to go to bed tired.

One afternoon at twilight he was walking round the reservoir in the Park when he recognized something familiar in a trim little figure approaching him—something that changed the beat of his heart. It was Miss Bennett. He stopped her, uncertain of his reception.

"Is that Mr. O'Bannon?" she said, staring up at him in the dim light.

The city beyond the bare trees had begun to turn into a sort of universal lilac mist, punctuated with yellow dots of light. It was too dark for Miss Bennett to see any change in O'Bannon's appearance, anything ravaged and worn, anything suggesting an abnormal strain. Miss Bennett, though kind and gentle, was not imaginative about turbulent, irregular emotions, such as she herself did not experience. She was not on the lookout for danger signals.

She did not feel unfriendly to O'Bannon. On the contrary she admired him. She could, as she said, see his side of it. She prided herself on seeing both sides of every question. She greeted him cordially as soon as she was sure it was he. He turned and walked with her. They had the reservoir to themselves.

Miss Bennett thought it more tactful not to refer to Lydia. She began talking about the beauty of the city. Country people always spoke as if all natural beauty were excluded from towns, but for her part—

O'Bannon suddenly interrupted her.

"Have you seen Miss Thorne lately?" he said in a queer, quick, low tone.

When Benny felt a thing she could always express it. This was fortunate for her because when she expressed it she relieved the acuteness of her own feeling. She very naturally, therefore, sought the right phrase, even sometimes one of an almost indecent poignancy, because the more poignantly she made the other person feel the more sure she could be of her own relief. Then, too, she was not sorry that O'Bannon should understand just what it was he had done—his duty, perhaps, but he might as well know the consequences.

"Have I seen her?" she exclaimed. "Oh, Mr. O'Bannon!" There was a pause as if it were too terrible to go on with, but of course she did go on. "I see her every week. She's like an animal in a trap. Perhaps you never saw one—in a trap, I mean. Lydia had a gray wolfhound once, and in the woods it strayed away and got caught in a mink trap. It was almost dead when we found it, but so patient and hopeless. She's getting to be like that—each week a little more patient than the week before—she who was never patient. Oh, Mr. O'Bannon, I feel sometimes as if I couldn't bear it—the way they've ground it out of her in a few months! She seems like an old woman in a lovely young woman's body. They haven't spoiled that—at least they haven't yet."

She wiped her eyes with a filmy handkerchief, and her step became brisker. She felt better. For a moment she had got rid of the pathos of the situation. O'Bannon, she saw, had taken up her burden. He walked along beside her silent for a few steps, and then suddenly took off his hat, murmured something about being late for an engagement and left her, disappearing down the steep slope of the reservoir.

He wandered restlessly up and down like a man in physical pain. No reality, he finally decided, could be as terrible as the visions which, with the help of Miss Bennett, his imagination kept calling before him. That night he took the train, and in the middle of the next morning arrived at the prison gates.

There was no difficulty about his seeing the prisoner. His explanation that he was passing by on his way to see the warden about one of the men prisoners was not required. The matron agreed readily to send for Lydia. It seemed to him a long time before she came. He stood staring out of the window, stray sentences leaping up in his mind—"not less than three nor more than seven

121

years"—"an animal in a trap"—"an old woman in a lovely young woman's body." He heard steps approaching and his pulses began to beat thickly and heavily. He turned round, and as he did so she fell at his feet.

The matron came in, running at the sound of her fall. O'Bannon picked her up limp as a rag doll in his arms and carried her back to her cell. Under most circumstances he would have noticed that the cell was bright and large, but now he only compared it, with a pang at his heart, to that large, luxurious, deserted bedroom of Lydia's in which he had once interviewed Evans.

The matron drove him away before Lydia recovered consciousness. He waited in the outer room, heard that she was perfectly well, and then took his miserable departure. He got back to New York late that night, and the next day he resigned his position as district attorney.

Eleanor read of his resignation first in the local paper, and came to his mother for an explanation; but Mrs. O'Bannon was as much surprised as anyone. Without acknowledging it, both women were frightened at the prospect of O'Bannon's attempting, without backing, to build up a law practice in New York. Both dreaded the effect upon him of failure. Both would have advised against his resigning his position. Perhaps for this very reason neither had been consulted.

The two women who loved him parted with specious expressions of confidence. Doubtless Dan would make a great success of it, they said. He was brilliant, and worked so hard.

122

CHAPTER XV

In the spring Lydia was transferred from the kitchen to the long, bright workroom. Here the women prisoners hemmed the blankets woven in the men's prison. Here they themselves wove the rag rugs for the floors, made up the house linen and their own clothes—Joseph's too—not only their prison clothes, but the complete outfit with which each prisoner was dismissed.

Lydia was incredibly awkward with the needle. It surprised the tall, thin assistant in charge of the workroom that anyone who had had what she described as advantages could be so grossly ignorant of the art of sewing. Lydia hardly knew on which finger to put her thimble and tied a knot in her thread like a man tying a rope. But it was her very inability that first woke her interest, her will. She did not like to be stupider than anyone else. Suddenly one day her little jaw set and she decided to learn how to sew. From that moment she began to adjust herself to prison life.

Lydia wondered, considering prisoners in the first grade are allowed to receive visits from their families once a week, and from others, with the approval of the warden, once a month, at the small number of visitors who came to the prison. Were all these women cast off by their families? Evans explained the matter to her, and Lydia felt ashamed that she had needed an explanation.

"It takes a man a week's salary—at a good job, too—from New York here and back."

Lydia did what was rare of her—she colored. For the first time in her life she felt ashamed, not so much of the privileges of money but of the ease with which she had always taken them. It came over her that this was one of the objects for which Mrs. Galton had once asked a subscription. A memory rose of the way in which in old days she used to dispose of her morning's mail when it came in on her flowered breakfast tray. Advertisements and financial appeals from unknown sources were twisted together by her vigorous fingers and tossed into the waste-paper basket. Mrs. Galton's might well have been among these.

She was horrified on looking back at her own lack of humanity. She might have guessed without going through the experience that prison life needed some alleviation. It meant a great deal to her to see Benny every week. Benny stood in the place of her family. She longed to hear of the outside world and her old friends. But she did not crave these visits with such passion as the imprisoned mothers craved a sight of their children.

Thought leading quickly to action in Lydia, she arranged through Miss Bennett, allowing it to be supposed to be Miss Bennett's enterprise, to finance the visits of families to the prison. Everyone rejoiced, as if it were a common benefit, over the visit of Muriel's mother and the beautiful auburn-haired daughter of the middle-aged real-estate operator. Lydia felt as if she had been outside the human race all her life and had just been initiated into it. She said something like this to Evans.

"Oh, Louisa, rich people don't know anything, do they?"

Evans tried to console her.

"If they want to they always can."

It was true, Lydia thought; she had not wanted to know. She had not wanted anything but her own way, irrespective of anyone else's. That was being criminal—to want your own way too much. That was all that these people about her had wanted—these forgers and defrauders—their own way, their own way. Though she still held her belief that the killing of Drummond had been an accident, she saw that the bribing of him had been wrong—the same streak in her, the same determination to have her own way. She thought of her father and all their early struggles, and how when she had believed that she was triumphing most over him she had been at her worst.

Her poor father! It was from him she had inherited her will, but he had learned in life, as she was now learning in prison, that the strongest will is the will that knows how to bend.

She thought a great deal about her father. He must have been terribly lonely sometimes. She had never given him anything in the way of affection. She had not really loved him, and yet she loved him now. Her heart ached with a palpable weight of remorse. He had been her only relation, and she had done nothing but fight and oppose and wound him. What a cruel, stupid creature she had been—all her life! And now it was too late. Her father was gone, so long ago she had almost forgotten him in one aspect. And then again it would seem as if he must still be somewhere, waiting to order her upstairs as he had when she was a child.

Only Benny was left—Benny whom she had so despised. Yet Benny would not need to go to prison in order to learn to respect other people's rights. Benny had been born knowing just what everyone else wanted—eager to get all men their hearts' desire.

Lydia was not religious by temperament. She had now none of the joy of a great revelation. But she had the courage, unsupported by any sense of a higher power, to look at herself as she was. She saw now that her relation to life had always been ugly, hostile, violent. Everyone who had ever loved her had been able to love through something beautiful in their own natures—in spite of all the unloveliness of hers. She thought not only of the relations she had missed, like the relation to her father, but of friendships she had lost, which she had deliberately broken in the hideous daily struggle to get her own way. She would never now renew that struggle. She had come in contact with something stronger than herself, of which the impersonal power of the law was only a visible symbol. She was not sure whether it had broken her or remade her, but it had given her peace—happiness she had never had—a peace which she believed she could preserve even when she went out of the sheltering routine of prison. The only feature of life which terrified and revolted her was the persisting individuality of Lydia Thorne. If there were only a charm other than death to free you from yourself! Sometimes she felt like a maniac chained to a mirror. Yet she knew that it was the long months of enforced contemplations that had saved her.

On Friday evening the inmates were allowed to dance in the assembly room—half theater, half chapel. In her effort to escape from herself Lydia went once to watch, and came again and again with increasing interest. It soon began to be rumored that she was a good dancer and knew new steps. The dances became dancing classes. Lydia, except for her natural impatience, was a born teacher, clear in her explanations and willing to work for perfection.

Evans, who had taken Lydia to so many balls in past years, smiled to see her laboring over the steps of some heavy grandmother or light-footed—and perhaps light-fingered—mulatto girl.

An evening suddenly came back to her. It was in New York. She had come downstairs about eleven o'clock with Miss Thorne's opera cloak and fan. There had been people to dinner, but they had all gone except Mr. Dorset, and he was being instructed in some new intricacy of the dance. Miss Bennett, who belonged to a generation that knew something about playing the piano, was making music for them. Evans, if she shut her eyes, could see Lydia as she was then, in a short blue brocade, trying to shove her partner into the correct step and literally shaking him when he failed to catch her rhythm. She was being far more patient with Muriel, holding her pale coffee-colored hands and repeating, "One-two, one-two; one-two-three-four. There, Muriel, you've got it!" Her face lit up with pleasure as she turned to Evans. "Isn't she quick at it, Louisa?"

Lydia's second spring in prison was well advanced when she was sent for by the matron. Such a summons was an event Lydia racked her brain to think what was coming—for good or evil. The matron's first question was startling. Did she know anything about baseball?

Did she? Yes, something. Her mind went back to a Fourth of July house party she had been to where a baseball game among the guests was a yearly feature. She and the matron discussed the possibilities of getting up two nines among the inmates. She suggested that there were books on the subject. A book would be provided. She felt touched and flattered at the responsibility put upon her, humbly eager to succeed.

The whole question began to absorb her. She studied it in the evening and thought about it during the day, considering the possibilities of her material, the relation of character to skill. Grace, a forger, was actually a better pitcher, but the woman who had killed her husband had infinitely more staying power.

All through that second summer she occupied herself, day and night, with the team, more and more as September drew to a close. For she knew that with the approaching expiration of her minimum sentence the parole board would consider her release. Freedom in all probability was near, and freedom is a disorganizing thought to prisoners. The peace she had gained in prison began to flow away as each day brought her nearer to release. She began to dream that she was already free, and to wake dissatisfied, with a trace of the same restless irritation of her first weeks. Could it be, she thought, that she had learned nothing after all? Could even the idea of returning to the old life change her back into the old detestable thing?

Prison authorities have learned that the last night in prison is more trying to a prisoner's morale than any other, except perhaps the first. Lydia found it so when her last night there came. She knew that she was to be set free early in the morning. Miss Bennett would be there, and they would take an early train to New York together. It was a certainty, she kept telling herself, a certainty on which she could rely, and yet she spent the entire night in an agony of fear and impatience. She would have been calmer if she had been waiting the hour of a prearranged escape. The darkness of night continued so long that it seemed as if some unheralded eclipse had done away with sunrise, and when at last the dawn began to color the window the hour between it and her release was nothing but a fevered anxiety.

She was hardly aware of Miss Bennett waiting for her in the matron's room—hardly aware of the matron herself, imperturbable as ever, bidding her good-by. Only the clang of the gate behind her quieted her. Only from outside the bars did she want to pause and look back at the prison as at an old friend.

It was a bright autumn morning. The wind was chasing

126

immense white clouds across the sky and scattering the leaves of the endless row of trees that stood like sentinels along the high wall.

Miss Bennett wanted to hurry across the street at once to the railroad station, although their train would not start for some time; she wanted to get away from the menace of that dark wall—a very perfect piece of masonry. But Lydia had seen it too long from the inside not to be eager to savor a view of it from without. She stared slowly about her like a tourist before some spectacle of awesome beauty. She looked down the alley between the trees and the wall to where on her left was the sharp clean corner of the stonework. She looked to her right, where as the wall rose higher she could see the little watchtower of the prison guard. Then she turned completely round and looked back through the bars at the prison itself.

"Don't you think it's a pretty old doorway?" she said.

Miss Bennett acknowledged its beauty rather briefly.

"Will you tell me why it has 'State Asylum' on the horse block?" she said.

"That's just what it is," said Lydia—"an asylum, a real asylum to some of us. It used to be for the insane, Benny. That's why."

On the all-day journey to New York Miss Bennett had counted on hearing the full psychological story of the last two years. In her visits to the prison she had found that Lydia wanted to hear of the outside world—not to talk of herself; but now that she was free Miss Bennett hoped this might be changed. She had taken a compartment so they could be by themselves, but the minute the door was shut upon them a funny change came over Lydia. She grew absent and tense, and at last she sprang up and opened it.

"It's pleasanter open," she said haughtily, and then she suddenly laughed. "Oh, Benny, to be able to open a closed door!"

Miss Bennett began to cry softly. All these months she had been trying to persuade herself that the change in Lydia was due to prison clothes; but now, seeing her dressed as she used to dress, the change was still there. She was thinner, finer—shaped, as it were, by a sharper mold. All her reactions were slower. It took her longer to answer, longer to smile. This gave her—what Lydia had never had before—a touch of mystery, as if her real life were going on somewhere else, below the surface, remote from companionship.

She wiped her eyes, thinking that she must not let Lydia guess she thought her changed. Their eyes met. Lydia was discovering a curious fact, which she in her turn thought it better to conceal. It was this: That the figures of her prison life had a depth and reality that made all the rest of the world seem like shadows. Even while she questioned Miss Bennett about her friends she felt as if she were asking about characters in a book which she had not had time to

127

finish. Would Bobby be sure to be at the station? Was Eleanor coming to town that night to see her? Where was Albee?

Miss Bennett did not know where Albee was, and her tone indicated that she did not greatly care. She did not intend to stir Lydia up against anyone but she could not help wishing Lydia would punish Albee. He had not been really loyal, and he was the only one of the intimate circle who had not been. A man with red blood in his veins, Miss Bennett thought, would have married Lydia the day before she went to prison or would at least be waiting, hat in hand, the day she came out.

Bobby, gay and affectionate as ever, met them at the station and drove with them to the town house. Morson opened the front door and ran down the steps with a blank face and a brisk manner, as if she had been returning from a week-end; but as she stepped out of the motor he attempted a sentence.

"Glad to see you back, miss," he said, and then his self-control gave way. He turned aside with one hand over his eyes and the other feeling wildly in his tail pocket for a handkerchief.

Lydia began to cry too. She put her hand on Morson's shoulder and said, "I'm so glad to see you, Morson. You're almost the oldest friend I have in the world," and she added, without shame, to Miss Bennett, "Isn't it awful the way I cry at anything nowadays?"

She went into the house, blowing her nose.

The house was full of telegrams and flowers. Lydia did not open the telegrams, but the flowers seemed to give her pleasure. She went about breathing in long whiffs of them and touching their petals. Morson, in perfect control of himself, but with his eyes as red as fire, came to ask at what hour she would dine.

Lydia had a great deal to do before dinner. She produced a dirty paper from her pocketbook and began studying it.

"Is there anything special you'd like to order?" said Miss Bennett.

Lydia did not look up but answered that Morson remembered what she liked, which drove him out of the room again. Her telephoning, it appeared, was to the families and friends of her fellow prisoners. She was very conscientious about it, and very patient, even with those who, unaccustomed to the telephone or unwilling to lose touch with a voice so recently come from their loved ones, would ask the same question over and over again.

But finally it was over, and Lydia free to bathe and dress and finally to sit down in her own dining room to a wonderful little meal that was the symbol of her freedom. Yet all she could think of was the smell of the freshly baked dinner rolls that brought back the large, low kitchen and the revolving oven—revolving at that very moment, perhaps—so far away.

"Oh, my dear," said Miss Bennett, "I've found the nicest little maid for you—a Swiss girl who can sew—really make your things if you want her to, and—"

Lydia felt embarrassed. She turned her head from side to side as Miss Bennett ran on describing the discovery. She simply could never have a maid again. How was she to explain? She did not understand it thoroughly herself, only she knew that she could never again demand that another woman—as young, perhaps, and as fond of amusement as herself—should give a lifetime to taking care of her wardrobe. Personal service like that would annoy and embarrass her now. The first thing to do was to make her life less complex in such matters. She put her hand over Miss Bennett's as it lay on the table.

"Shouldn't you think she'd wish me back at hard labor?" she said to Bobby. "She takes such a lot of trouble for me."

Miss Bennett, emotionally susceptible to praise, wiped her eyes, and presently went away, leaving Bobby and Lydia alone. She wondered if perhaps that would be the best thing for Lydia to do—to rebuild her life on Bobby's gay but unwavering devotion.

Lydia, leaning her elbows on the table and her chin on her hands, listened while Bobby gossiped over the empty coffee cups. Did Lydia know about this Western coal man that May Swayne was going to marry? Bobby set him before her in an instant—"A round-faced man, Lydia, with $30,000,000, and such a vocabulary! He never thinks; he presumes. He doesn't come into a room; he ventures to intrude. May has quite a lot of alterations to do on him."

And the Piers—had Lydia heard about them? Fanny had fallen in love with the prophet of a new religion and had made all her arrangements to divorce Noel, but before she left him, as a proof of her new powers, she thought she'd cure him of drinking. Well, my dear, she did. And the result was she found she liked a nonalcoholic Noel better than ever—and she chucked the seer. Can you beat it?

Shadows—they did seem like shadows to Lydia. Staring before her, she fell into meditation, remembering Evans and the pale coffee-colored Muriel and the matron—the small, placid-browed matron who knew not fear.

Suddenly she came back to realize that Bobby was asking her to marry him.

Most of their acquaintances believed that he never did anything else; but as a matter of fact, it was the first time he had ever put it into words. He wasn't sure it was a tactful thing to do now. She might think—Bobby was always terribly aware of what

129

people might think—that his suggesting such a mediocre future for her was to admit that he thought her beaten. Whereas to him she was as triumphant and desirable as ever. On the other hand, it might be just the right thing to do. With men like Albee getting to cover and some people bound to be hateful, she could say to herself, "Well, I can always marry Bobby and go to live in Italy."

He put it to her.

"Lydia, wouldn't you consider marrying me to-morrow and sailing for Greece or Sicily or Grenada—that's a heavenly place. I should be so wildly happy, dear, that I think you'd be pleased in a mild sort of way, too."

Go away? It was the last thing she wanted to do.

"No, no!" she said quickly. "I must stay here!"

"Well, marry me and stay here."

She shook her head, trying to explain to him—she wouldn't ever marry. She had found a new clew to life and wanted to follow it alone. She had interest, intense, vital interest, to give to life and affairs—yes, and even people; but she had not love. Human relationships couldn't make or mar life for her any more. She wanted to work—nothing else.

She paused, and in the pause the dining-room door opened and Eleanor came in. Eleanor had been up at dawn to get a train from the Adirondacks in time to meet Lydia at the station, and of course the train had been late. Would Lydia put her up for the night?

Lydia's cry of welcome did not sound like a person to whom all human relationships had become indifferent. Indeed Eleanor was the person she wanted most to see. Eleanor was not emotional, or rather she expressed her emotion by a heightened intellectual sensitiveness. She wouldn't cry, she wouldn't regard Lydia as a shorn lamb the way Miss Bennett did, nor yet would she assume that she was utterly unchanged, as all the rest of her friends might. Eleanor's manner was almost commonplace. Perhaps it would be fairer to say that she left the introduction of anything dramatic to Lydia's choice.

Bobby soon went away and left the two women together. They went upstairs to Lydia's bedroom, and in their dressing gowns, with chairs drawn to the fire, they talked. They talked with long pauses between them. No one but Eleanor would have allowed those long silences to pass uninterrupted, but she was wise enough to know they were the very essence of companionship.

Though Eleanor asked several questions about the details of prison life, she was too wise to ask anything about the fundamental change which she felt had taken place in Lydia. She did not betray

130

that she felt there was a change. She wondered whether Lydia knew it herself. It was hard to say, for the girl, always inexpert with verbal expressions, had become more so in the two years of solitude and contemplation. Whatever spontaneity of speech she had had was gone. She was, Eleanor thought, like a person using an unfamiliar tongue, aware of the difficulty of putting thought into words.

She could not help being touched—and a little amused—at the seriousness with which Lydia mentioned her late companions; Lydia, who had always been so selective about her own friends and so scornful about everybody else's. She spoke of Evans, the pallid little thief, as if light had flowed from her as from an incarnation of the Buddha. Seeing that Lydia had caught some reflection of the thought, Eleanor thought it better to put it into words.

"Now, don't tell me, my dear," she said, "that you, too, have discovered that all criminals are pure white souls."

"Just the opposite. All pure white souls are criminals—all of us are criminals at heart. The only way not to be is to recognize the fact that you are. It's a terrible idea at first—at least it was to me. It was like going through death and coming out alive." Lydia paused, staring before her, and anyone in the world except Eleanor would have thought she had finished; but Eleanor's fine ear caught the beat of an approaching idea. "But it's such a comfort, Nell, to belong to the tribe—such a relief. And I should never have had it if it had not been"—she hesitated, and Eleanor's heart contracted with a sudden fear that the name of O'Bannon was about to enter—"if it had not been for my accident."

Eleanor was not sure that Lydia had deliberately avoided the name. What, she wondered, was left of that unjust and bitter hatred? She could not detect a trace of bitterness anywhere in Lydia's nature to-night. But then she had always had those moments of gentleness.

Presently Miss Bennett came in to say in her old, timid, suggestive manner that it was late—she hated to interrupt them, but she really did think that Lydia ought to go to bed. Lydia got up at once.

"I suppose I ought," she said. "It's been an exciting day for me."

Eleanor noted that such a suggestion from Miss Bennett in old days would have meant that Lydia would have felt it her duty to stay up another hour.

"I have to, my dear," she would have said, "or else Benny would be trying to coerce me in every detail of my life."

131

CHAPTER XVI

The next morning at the regular prison hour Lydia woke with a start. She had been aware for some time of a strange unaccountable roaring in her ears. She looked about her, surprised to see that the light of dawn was not falling through a tall barred aperture at the head of her bed, but was coming across a wide carpeted room from two chintz-curtained windows. Then she remembered she was at home; the roaring was the habitual sound of a great city; the room was the room she had had since she was a child. It seemed less familiar to her, less homelike, than her cell. She put out her hand to the satin coverlet and the sheets, softer than satin. The physical sensation of the contact was delicious, and yet there was something sad about it too. It was the thought of her late companions that made her sad, as if she had deserted them in trouble.

It would be two hours or more before Eleanor and Benny would be awake. She flung her arms above her head and lay back, thinking. She mustn't let them cherish her as if she were a wounded, stricken creature. She was more to be envied now than in the old fighting days, when all her inner life had been a sort of poisoned turmoil. No one had pitied her then.

Her plan had been not to be too hasty in arranging her new life, which she knew must include work—work in connection with prisoners. But now she saw she mustn't waste a minute. She must have work at once to take her away from herself. She could hardly face the coming day—everyone considering her and that detestable ego of hers, asking her what she wanted to do. She must have a routine immediately. She was not strong enough yet to live without one. Only one thing must take precedence of everything else—a pardon for Evans. She could not bear to remain at liberty with Evans still serving a sentence. With that accomplished, she could go forward in peace. In peace? As she thought of it she knew that there was one corner of her mind where there was not and never would be peace. Only last evening, in the first happiness of being at home, the mention of O'Bannon's name had threatened to destroy it.

And now he was in her mind, holding it without rivals. The moment had come when her hatred of him could find expression. It needn't be a secret dream, like a child's fairy story. She needn't suppress it—she could act. If she had not been such a coward last evening she would have named him and gone boldly on and found out from Eleanor where he was, what he was doing, what was his

132

heart's desire. Perhaps if she had put her questions frankly Eleanor would not have told her; but it would not be difficult to deceive so doting a friend of his. Eleanor could easily be persuaded that his victim had been so tamed and crushed in prison that she had come to admire him, to look differently on the world.

Suddenly Lydia sat straight up in her bed. And hadn't she changed? In the old days she had never felt with more bitter violence than she was feeling now. The excitement of her revenge had wiped out every other interest. The flame of her hatred had destroyed the whole structure of her new philosophy. She sat up in her bed and wrung her hands. What could she do? What could she do? The mere thought of that man changed her back into being the woman she hated to be. She would rather die than live as her old self, but how could she help thinking of him when the idea of injuring him was more vivid, more exciting, than any other idea in the world? She had come out of prison resolved that her first action would be to get a pardon for Evans, and here she was forgetting her obligations and her remorse, forgetting everything but a desire to wound and destroy. He had the power to make her what she loathed to be.

Her room was at the back of the house, and the sun, finding some chink between the houses behind the Thorne house, crept in under the shades and began moving slowly across the plain, dark, velvet carpet. It had time to move some distance while she sat there immovable, unaware of her surroundings.

Gradually she came to see that she must choose between the two. Either she must give up forever the idea of revenging herself on O'Bannon or she must give up all the peace and wisdom that she had so painfully learned—she had almost lost it already, and she had not been twenty-four hours out of prison.

An hour later Eleanor was wakened by the opening of her door. Lydia was standing at the foot of her bed, grasping the edge of it in her two white hands. It was Eleanor's first good look at her in the light of day. She was startled by Lydia's beauty—a kind of beauty she had never had before. No one could now have likened her to a picture by Cabanel of the Star of the Harem. Everything sleek and hard and smooth had gone. She looked more like the picture of some ravaged, pale Spanish saint, still so young that the inner struggle had molded without lining her face. She stood staring at Eleanor, her dark hair standing out about her face, and her pale dressing gown defining the beautiful line of her shoulders, as she raised them, pressing her hands down on the foot of the bed.

"Well, my dear, good morning," was Eleanor's greeting,

133

though she was not unaware that something emotional was in the air.

"Eleanor," began the other, her enormous tragic eyes fixed now, not on her friend's, but on a spot on the pillow about five inches away, "there is something I want to say to you." The best agreement was silence, and Lydia went on, "I want you never to talk to me about that man—your friend—I mean O'Bannon."

"Talk of him!" exclaimed Eleanor, her first thought being, "Am I always talking of him?"

"I don't want to hear of him or think of him or speak of him."

This time Eleanor's hesitation was not entirely acquiescent.

"I can understand," she said, "that you might not want to see him, but to speak of him—I have been thinking, Lydia, that that is one of the subjects that you and I ought to talk over—to talk out."

"No, no!" returned Lydia quickly, and Eleanor saw with surprise that it was only by leaning on her hands that she kept them from trembling. "I can't explain it to you—I don't want to go into it—but I don't want to remember that he exists. If you would just accept it as a fact, and tell other people—Benny and Bobby. If you would do that for me, Eleanor—"

"Of course I'll do it," answered Eleanor. There really was not anything else to say. The next instant Lydia was gone.

Eleanor lay quite still, trying to understand the meaning of the scene. She was often accused by her friends of coldness, of lack of human imagination, of attempting to substitute mental for emotional processes. Aware of a certain amount of justice in these accusations, she tried to atone by putting her reasoning faculty most patiently and gently at work upon the problems of those she loved. Her nature was not capable of really understanding turgidity, but she did better than most people inasmuch as she avoided forming wrong judgments about it. She felt about Lydia now as she had once felt when O'Bannon had described to her his struggle against drinking—wonder that a person so much braver and stronger than she, Eleanor, was, could be content to avoid temptation instead of fighting it.

At breakfast, which the three women had together, Eleanor saw that Lydia had regained her calm of the evening before. While they were still at table Wiley was shown in. He felt obviously a certain constraint, an embarrassment to know what to say, which he concealed under a formal professional manner. Lydia put a stop to this simply enough by getting up and putting her arms round his neck.

"I've thought so much of all you've been doing for me since I was a child," she said.

134

He was associated in her mind with her father. Wiley felt his eyelids stinging.

"Why, my dear child, my dear child!" he said. And he held her off to look at her as if uncertain that it was the same girl. "Well, I must say prison doesn't seem to have done you much harm."

"It's done me good, I hope," said Lydia.

She made him sit down and drink an extra cup of coffee. There was something quite like a festival in the comradeship that developed among the four of them. She began to question her visitor about the method of getting a pardon for Evans. He advised her to go and see Mrs. Galton. At the name she and Benny glanced at each other and smiled. They were both thinking of the day when Lydia had so resented the presence of the old lady in her house.

She went to Mrs. Galton's office that same morning. It occupied the second floor of an old building that looked out over Union Square. Lydia had not thought of making an appointment, and when she reached the outer office she was told that Mrs. Galton was engaged—would be engaged for some time—a member of the parole board was in conference. Would Miss Thorne wait?

Yes, Lydia would wait. She sat down on a hard bench and watched the work of the society go on before her eyes. She had some knowledge of business and finance, and she knew very soon that she was in the presence of an efficient organization; but it was not only the efficiency that charmed her—it was partly the mere business routine, which made her feel like coming home after she had been at sea. The clear impersonal purpose of it all promised forgetfulness of self. At the end of half an hour of waiting she was possessed with the desire to become part of this work. Here was the solution of her problem. When at last she was shown into Mrs. Galton's bleak little office—not half the size of Lydia's cell—her first words were not of Evans, after all.

"Mrs. Galton," she said, "can you use me in this organization?"

Without intending the smallest disrespect to Mrs. Galton, it must be admitted that this question was like asking a lion if it could use a lamb. The organization, like all others of its type, needed devotion, needed workers, needed money, and was not averse to a little discreet publicity. All these Lydia offered. Mrs. Galton smiled.

"Yes," she said. The monosyllable was expressive.

The older woman, with forty years of executive work behind her, divided all workers roughly into two classes: The amiable idealists who created no antagonism and accomplished nothing, and the effective workers who accomplished marvels and stirred up endless quarrels. She—except in her very weakest moments—

135

preferred the latter, though they disrupted her office force and gave her nervous indigestion. She recognized Lydia as belonging to this class.

And presently, being a wise and experienced woman, she recognized another fact: That she was probably in the presence of her successor. A pang shot through her. She was seventy and keener than ever about the work to which she had given all her life. If she kept this girl out she would hold office longer than if she let her in. If she let her in it would vivify the whole organization. She might become the ideal leader; at least she could be made so—youth, beauty, money, experience of prison conditions and the romance of her story to capture public imagination.

Lydia, with her acute sense of her own unworthiness, was dimly aware of some hesitation, and supposed that she was being weighed in the balance. She had no suspicion that a struggle, somewhat like her own struggle, was going on in the honest, philanthropic breast before her. A few minutes afterwards Mrs. Galton offered her the treasurership. Lydia was overcome by the honor.

"But I thought you had a treasurer, already," she murmured. "If I could be her assistant—"

"Oh, no doubt she will be glad to resign," said the president with a calmness that suggested that glad or not the resignation would be forthcoming.

The two women went out to lunch together. More and more, as they talked, Lydia saw that this was just what she wanted. This would be her salvation. After they were back in the office again she spoke of Evans. What could she do? What must be done?

"Let me see," said Mrs. Galton. "You were the complaining witness against her, I suppose. Well, you must see the judge and the district attorney who tried the case."

Lydia gave a funny little sound, half exclamation, half moan.

"O'Bannon!" she said.

No, Mrs. Galton thought that wasn't the name of the district attorney of Princess County. She rang her bell and told her secretary to look it up, while she went on calmly discussing the details of the procedure. Presently the secretary returned with a book. John J. Hillyer was district attorney.

"Are you sure?" Lydia asked. "I thought Mr. O'Bannon was."

The secretary said, consulting her book, that he had resigned almost two years before.

"But we'd have to have his signature, wouldn't we?" said Mrs. Galton.

She and the secretary talked of it, back and forth, not knowing

136

that they were setting an impossible condition for Lydia. She couldn't ask O'Bannon. All her interest in the prospect of this new work had withered at the name. She felt a profound discouragement. It was terrible to find she would rather leave Evans in prison than ask O'Bannon to help get her out; terrible to find that man like a barrier across every path she tried to follow in order to escape from him. She thanked them for the trouble they had taken and rose to go. It was arranged that she was to come and begin work on the following Monday.

It was almost tea time when she reached home. Bobby was there, and the Piers, and presently May Swayne came in with her coal baron. Lydia's first emotion on seeing them was a warm, welcoming gladness, but she soon found to her surprise that she had very little to say to them.

The truth was that she had lost the trick of meeting her fellow beings in a purely social relation, and the conscious effort to adapt herself, her words, her attention to them exhausted her. She looked back with wonder to the old days, when she had done nothing else all day long.

Miss Bennett soon began to notice that she was looking like a little piece of carved ivory, with eyes of the blackest jet. When at last her visitors had all gone she went straight to bed.

The next day she had herself driven down to Wide Plains, so that she could see Judge Homans. Court was still in session when she got there, and she was shown to the judge's little book-lined room and left to wait. She had expected her first view of the wide main street, of Mr. Wooley's shop, of the columned courthouse to be intensely painful to her, but it wasn't. The tall attendant who ushered her in greeted her warmly. She remembered him clearly leaning against the double doors of the court room to prevent anyone leaving during the judge's charge.

Presently the judge came in, just as he had come in every day to her trial, his hands folded, his robes flowing about him. Lydia rose. Her name apparently had not been given to him, for he looked at her in surprise. Then his face lit up.

"My dear Miss Thorne," he said, "when did you get out?"

It was the first perfectly natural, spontaneous reference to her imprisonment that she had heard since she left prison. It did away with all constraint and awkwardness, to be taken as a matter of course. Criminals were no novelty in the judge's life. He sat down, waved her into a chair opposite, put his elbows on the arms of his swinging chair and locked his knuckles together.

"I'm very glad to see you—very glad indeed," he said.

But he wasn't at all surprised that she had come. It was not

137

unusual, evidently, for the first visit of a released convict to be paid to the judge. He began to question her rather as if she were a child home for the holidays.

"And what did you learn? Baking? Now that's interesting, isn't it? And sewing? Well, well!"

He treated her so simply that Lydia found herself speaking to him with more freedom about the whole experience of prison than she had been able to speak to anyone. The reason was, she thought, that she did not need to explain to him that she was not a tragic exception, a special case. To him she was just one of a long series of lawbreakers.

They talked for an hour. She noted that the judge still enjoyed talking, still insisted on rounding out his sentences; but she felt now no impatience. His reminiscences interested her. Before long she found herself consulting him about a subject that had long preyed on her mind—Alma Wooley. She wanted to do something for Alma Wooley, yet she supposed the girl would utterly reject anything coming from the woman who had—

The judge put his hand on her arm.

"Now don't you worry a mite about Alma," he said. "Alma married a nice young fellow out of the district attorney's office—named Foster—and now they have a baby, a nice little baby. I was saying to her father only yesterday that Foster is a much better man for her—"

While the judge was launched on his speech to Mr. Wooley, Lydia's mind went back to Foster—Foster waiting and watching for O'Bannon like a puppy for its supper. Well, she could forgive him even his admiration for that man since he had made Alma Wooley happy. A weight was lifted from her conscience.

Finally, with some embarrassment, she told the judge the object of her visit—a pardon for Evans. She was prepared to have him remind her, as O'Bannon had once done, that it was a matter which had been in her own hands, in that in this very room in which she was now sitting she had virtually refused to help Evans. But Judge Homans, if he remembered, made no reference to the past.

"Yes, yes," he said. "Now let me see. It must have been O'Bannon tried that case, wasn't it?" Lydia nodded, and he went on, "Poor O'Bannon! I miss him very much. He resigned, you know, about the time Mrs. O'Bannon died."

"He was married?" asked Lydia, and even in her own ears her voice sounded unnaturally loud.

No, the judge said, it was the old lady, his mother; and he went on telling Lydia what a fine fellow the former district attorney had been—a good man and a good lawyer.

138

"The two are not always combined," the judge said with a chuckle, feeling something cold in his auditor's attention.

Lydia rose to her feet. She was sorry, she said, that she really must be going home. The judge found his soft black hat and accompanied her to her car.

"Don't drive yourself?" he asked.

She shook her head. She would never drive a car again. The judge patted her hand—told her to come and see him again—let him know how she was getting on. She promised. She saw that in some way an unbreakable human bond had been established between them by the fact that she had committed a crime and he had sentenced her to state's prison for it.

She went home feeling encouraged. Not only had she managed to get him to agree to enlist O'Bannon's help in the matter of Evans' pardon, but she herself had supported the mention of O'Bannon's name with something that was almost calm.

CHAPTER XVII

It was noticeable—though no one noticed it—that a month after Lydia went to work in Mrs. Galton's organization everyone in her immediate circle was doing something for released convicts. Bobby, Miss Bennett, Eleanor, Wiley, all suddenly began to think that the problem of the criminal was the most important, the most vital, the most interesting problem in the world. The explanation was simple: A will like Lydia's, harnessed to a constructive purpose, was far more irresistible than in the old days when it had been selfish, spasmodic and undisciplined.

She was given a little office, like Miss Galton's, and she was in it every morning at nine o'clock. Miss Bennett, who had worried all her life because Lydia led an irregular, aimless, idle existence, now worried even more because her working hours were long.

"Surely," she protested almost every morning, "Mrs. Galton will not care if you don't get there until half past nine or even ten. These cold days it isn't good for you—"

Lydia explained that she was not going to the office early in order to please Mrs. Galton, who, as a matter of fact, did not arrive there until late in the morning. The organization needed money desperately, there was much to be done. But the truth was she loved the routine—the hard impersonal work. It saved her from herself. She was almost happy.

Eleanor had evidently done what she had been asked to do, for O'Bannon seemed to have dropped out of the world. His name was never mentioned, and as week after week went by it seemed to Lydia that she herself was forgetting him. Perhaps a time would come when she could even see him without wrecking her peace of soul. Her only sorrow was the delay in Evans' pardon. It didn't come. Lydia could not enjoy her liberty with Evans in prison. The forms had all been complied with, but the governor did not act. At last Mrs. Galton suggested her going to Albany; or perhaps she knew someone who would have influence with the governor. Yes, Lydia knew someone—Albee.

Albee was now senator from his own state, and a busy session in Washington had kept him there. He had been among the first to telegraph Lydia. She found his message and his flowers in the house when she first came home. The message sounded as if it had come from a friend; but Lydia knew that it had not; that Albee had escaped from her and her influence, or thought he had. She had known it even in the days of her trial, and looking back on the facts and on herself she wondered that she had not resented it. Those were days in which she had awarded punishments readily, and Albee had really behaved badly to her. They had been very nearly engaged and yet the instant she was in trouble he had deserted her. He had gone through all the motions of helping her, but in spirit she knew that Albee the day she killed Drummond had begun to disentangle himself. She felt not the least resentment against him; only she recognized the fact that his remoteness from her made it more difficult to make use of him for Evans, unless—the idea suddenly came to her—it might make it easier. He would avoid seeing her if he could; but if she found her way to him he might be eager to atone, to set himself right by doing her a definite favor.

The evening of the day that she saw this clearly she took a train to Washington. The next morning she was waiting in his outer office before he reached it himself. A new secretary—the old one had been promoted to some position of political prominence at home—did not know her and had not been warned against her by name. So she was sitting there when Albee came in with his old cheerful, dominating, leonine look. Just for the fraction of a second his face fell at seeing her, and then he hurried to her side, as if out of all the world she was the person he most wanted to see.

It must not be supposed that Lydia had become so saintly that she had forgotten her knowledge of men. She knew now that if she were cordial to Albee she could not depend on his doing what she wanted. If on the other hand she withheld her friendship she was sure he would bid high for it. She ignored all his flustered protestations. She smiled at him, a smile a little sad, a little chilly and infinitely remote.

"I want very much to speak to you, Stephen," she said, and her tone told him that whatever she wanted to talk about had nothing whatsoever to do with themselves.

He led her into the inner office. A curious thing was happening to him. He had never been in love with Lydia. He had deliberately allowed her beauty and wealth to dazzle him; he had admired her courage, her sureness of herself, contrasting it with his own terror of giving offense to anyone; but at times he had almost hated her. If she had inspired him with one atom of tenderness he would not have deserted her. She never had. He had cut himself off from her without regret. But now as she sat there, finer and paler and more—much more—than two years older, she did inspire tenderness, tenderness of a most vivid and disturbing sort. He could not take his eyes from her face. He suddenly cut into what she was saying about Evans.

141

"Lydia, my dear, are you happy? Yes, yes, of course I can get from the governor anything you ask me, but tell me about yourself."

He leaned over, taking her hands in his. She rose, withdrawing them slowly as she did so.

"Not now," she answered, and moved toward the door.

"You mustn't go like that," he protested. "Just think, my dear, I have not seen you for two years—the toughest two years I ever spent! You can't just come and go like this. I must see you, talk to you."

"When you have got me Evans' pardon, Stephen—if you get it." She still spoke gently, but there was a good deal of intention behind Lydia at her gentlest.

He caught the "if"—almost an insult after his confident assertion, but he did not think of the insult. He was aware of nothing but the desire that she should smile gayly and admiringly at him again as she used to, making him feel Jovian.

"I'm going to New York on Thursday," he said. "On Friday evening you shall have the pardon. Will you be at the opera Friday evening?"

She hesitated. She had not been to the opera yet. She could not bear the publicity of that blazing circle, but she had kept her box. After all, she thought, she could sit in the back of it, and music was one of the greatest of her pleasures.

"Will you join me there?" she said.

"It will be like old times."

"Not quite," she answered.

Still with his hand on the knob of the door, as if he were just going to open it for her, he detained her, trying to make her talk, asking her about her friends, her work, her health; trying to hit upon the master key to her mind, and at last, for he was a man of long experience, he found it.

"And that damned crook who prosecuted your case," he said. "Do you ever see him?"

She shook her head.

"I prefer not even to think of him," she replied, and this time she made a gesture that he should open the door. Instead he stepped in front of it. He had waked her; he had her attention at last.

"Naturally, naturally," he said, "but I wish you would think of him for a minute. I'm in rather a fix about that fellow."

She longed to know what the fix was, but she did not dare hear. She said softly, "Please don't make me think of him, Stephen. I'd really rather not."

142

"But you must listen, Lydia. Help me. I don't know what I ought to do. I have it in my power to ruin that man. Shall I?"

There was a pause. Albee heard her long breaths trembling as she drew them. He thought to himself that his knowledge of her had not gone astray. She had hated that man, and whatever else had changed in her, that hadn't. She suddenly came to life and tried to open the door for herself.

"I must go," she said. He did not move.

"You know," he said, speaking quickly, "that after your trial he went to pieces, resigned his position, took to drinking again, tried to make his way in New York. He was nearly down and out for a time there."

He watched her. A smile, a terrible smile, began to curve the corners of her mouth. He went on:

"I couldn't be exactly sorry for his bad luck. In fact, to be candid, I gave him a kick or two when I had the chance. But now he's pulled himself out. He's worked like a dog, and I hear that a couple of friends of mine, of the firm of Simpson, Aspinwall & McCarter, are going to offer him a partnership. It's a big firm, particularly in the political world." There was a short silence. "Shall I let him have it, Lydia?"

She raised her shoulders scornfully.

"Could you stop his getting it, Stephen?"

"Do you doubt it?"

She turned on him. Her jaw was set and lifted as in the old days.

"Of course I do! If you could have you certainly would have without consulting me. There is a man who you know lacks all integrity and honor, and who, moreover, goes about saying that you tried to bribe him—and failed. Oh, he makes a great point of that— you failed! Would you let a man like that go into a firm of your friends if you could stop it? No, no! Not unless you have grown a good deal meeker than I remember you, Stephen."

Albee made a sweeping gesture, as expressive as a Roman emperor's thumbs down.

"He shall not have it," and he added with a smile as cruel as Lydia's own: "He believes himself absolutely sure of it."

She smiled straight into his eyes.

"Bring me that Friday night," she said. "It's more important than the pardon."

He opened the door for her and she went out.

This was Wednesday. She could hardly wait for Friday to come. This was the right way—to destroy the man first and then to forget him. She had been silly and sentimental and weak to fancy

143

that she could have real peace in any other way, to imagine that she could go through life skulking, fearing. She was furious at herself when she remembered that she had asked Eleanor to avoid mentioning his name. She could mention his name now herself, and see him too. She would enjoy seeing him. She was hardly aware of the passage of time on her journey back to New York. She was living over a meeting between O'Bannon and herself after the partnership had been withdrawn. He must be made aware that it was her doing.

She reached home just before dinner, and found that Miss Bennett was dining out. Good! Lydia had no objection to being alone. But Benny had arranged otherwise. She had telephoned to Eleanor, and she was coming to dine. Lydia smiled. That was pleasant too.

Eleanor was an intelligent woman but not a mind reader. She saw some change had taken place in Lydia, noticed that she ate no dinner, and came to the conclusion that something had gone wrong about Evans' pardon; that Albee had been, as usual, a weak friend. When they were alone after dinner was over she prepared herself to hear the story. Instead, Lydia said, "I'm going to the opera on Friday, Nell—Samson and Delilah. Will you come with me?"

There was a little pause, a slight constraint. Then Eleanor answered that she couldn't; that she had a box of her own that someone had sent her. Lydia sprang up with a sudden, short, wild laugh.

"That man's going with you!" she said.

"Mr. O'Bannon? Yes, he is." Eleanor thought a second. "I'll put him off, Lydia. I'll tell him not to come."

"You'll do nothing of the kind. It's perfect. I don't know what got into me the other day, Eleanor. You must have despised me for such pitiful cowardice."

"No, my dear," said Eleanor slowly, but obviously relieved that the question had come up again. "But I did feel that you weren't going to work the best way to get the poison of the whole thing out of your soul."

Lydia laughed the same way again.

"Oh, don't worry about that! I shall get rid of the poison."

"How?"

"I shall make him suffer. I shall revenge myself, and then forget he exists. You can tell him so if you want."

Eleanor stared in front of her, blank and serious. Then she said, "I don't have many opportunities any more. I seldom see him."

Lydia's eyes brightened.

"Ah, you've found him out!"

"On the contrary, the longer I know him the more highly I

144

think of him. I don't see him because he's busy. He has been having a difficult time—in business. He decided to get out of politics and go into straight law. New York is like a ferocious monster to a man beginning any profession. Dan—but it doesn't matter. His troubles are over now."

"Are they indeed?" said Lydia.

"Yes, he's had a wonderful offer of a partnership from an older man who—Oh, Lydia, you ought to try to see that your point of view about him is a prejudiced—a natural one, but still—"

"Is it a definite offer, Eleanor?"

"Yes, absolutely, though the papers are not to be signed for a day or so."

Lydia breathed in thoughtfully "A day or so," and Eleanor pressed on.

"It isn't that I care what you think of him or he of you. I'm past that with my friends, and, as I say, I don't see nearly as much of him as I used to; but—"

"Of course you don't," answered Lydia. "He's ashamed—or, no, it's more that he can't bear to see himself in contrast with your perfect integrity, Eleanor. Did you know that he came to prison to see me, to gloat over me? Sent in for me to come to him in my prison clothes—"

Lydia's breath quickened as she spoke of the outrage.

"He didn't come to gloat over you."

"What did he come for then?"

To her own surprise Eleanor heard her own voice saying, as if unaided it tapped some source of knowledge never before open to her, "Because you know very well, Lydia, the man's in love with you."

Lydia sprang forward like a cat.

"Never say such a thing as that again!" she said. "You don't understand, but it degrades me, it pollutes me! Love me! That man! I'd kill him if I thought he dared!"

Nothing rendered Eleanor so calm as excitement in others.

"Well," she said, "perhaps I'm mistaken," and appeared to let the matter drop; but the other would not have it.

"Of course you're mistaken! But you must have had some reason for saying such a thing. You're not the kind of person, Eleanor, who goes about having disgusting suspicions like that without a reason."

"Do you really want me to give you a reason or are you only waiting to tear me to pieces, whatever I say?"

Lydia sat down and caught her hands between her knees, determined to be good.

145

"I want your reason," she said.

Reasons were not so easy, Eleanor found. She spoke slowly.

"I saw all through your trial that Dan was not like himself, that he was struggling with something stronger than he. He is a man who has always had terrible weaknesses, temptations—"

"He drinks," said Lydia, and there was a note of almost boastful triumph in her tone.

"No"—Eleanor was very firm about it—"in recent years only once."

"More than once, Eleanor."

"Only once, in a time of emotional strain. What was the emotion? You had just been sentenced. It came to me suddenly that if he were in love with you—it would explain everything."

"If he hated me—that would explain it too."

"The two emotions are pretty close, Lydia."

"Close?" Lydia exclaimed violently. "It shows that you have never felt either."

"Have you?"

"Yes, I've felt hate. It's poisoned and withered me for over two years now, and I don't mean to bear it any more. I mean to get rid of it this way—to hurt that man enough to satisfy myself."

Eleanor rose slowly, and the two women stood a little apart, looking at each other. Then Eleanor said, "You'll never get rid of it that way. Don't do it, Lydia, whatever you mean to do."

"You're pleading for that man, Nell. Don't! It's ignominious."

"I'm pleading for you, my dear."

"Don't! It's impertinent."

Worse than either, Eleanor knew it was useless. Her motor was waiting for her and she went away. For the first time she understood something that Dorset had once said to her—that Lydia in her evil moods was the most pathetic figure in the world.

146

Before the lights went up on the first entr'acte Lydia retreated to the little red-lined box of an anteroom and sank down on the red-silk sofa. She and Miss Bennett had come alone to the opera; but Dorset and Albee, who was committed to some sort of political dinner first, were to join them presently.

Even while the house was still in darkness Lydia had recognized the outline of O'Bannon's head in a box across the house. She had seen it before she had seen Eleanor. Miss Bennett had stayed in the front of the box. Lydia was glad she had. She wanted to be alone while she waited. She could see her between the curtains, sweeping the house with her opera glasses.

The door of the box opened and Albee came in. She did not speak, but looking up at him every muscle in her body grew tense with interest. He smiled at her and began to hang up his hat and take off his coat. She couldn't bear the suspense.

"Well?" she asked sternly.

"It's all right. The governor will sign it. It's only been pressure of business—"

She interrupted him.

"And the other thing? Have you failed there?" Somehow she had never thought of his failing. What should she do if he had?

He made a quick pass with his right hand, indicating that O'Bannon had been obliterated.

"Our friend will never be a partner in that firm," he said.

He looked at her eagerly and got his reward. She smiled at him, slowly wagging her head at the same time, as if he were too wonderful for words.

"Stephen, you are superb," she said, and evidently felt it. "Does he know it yet?"

"No, he won't know it until he opens his mail to-morrow morning."

Lydia leaned forward and peered out into the house between the curtains. Then she turned back and smiled again, but this time with amusement.

"He's over there now with Eleanor, pleased to death with himself and thinking the world is his oyster."

Albee had been standing. Now as the lights began to sink for the opening of the second act he gave an exclamation of annoyance.

"I have something to show you," he said. He sat down beside her on the narrow little sofa, and lowering his voice to fit the lowered lights he whispered, "What would you give for a copy of Simpson's letter withdrawing his partnership offer?"

"You have it?" Her voice betrayed that she would give anything.

"What would you give me for it?" he murmured, and in the darkness he put his arms about her and tried to draw her to him.

"I won't give you a thing!" Her voice was like steel, and so was her body.

Albee's heart failed him. It seemed as if his arms were paralyzed. He did not dare do what he had imagined himself doing—crushing her to him whether she consented or not. He suddenly thought to himself that she was capable of making an outcry.

"The inhuman, unfeminine creature!" he thought, even as he still held her.

He felt her put out her hand and quietly take the letter from him. No, that was a little too much! He caught her wrist and held it firmly. Then the door opened, someone came in, Bobby's voice said, "Are you here, Lydia?"

"Yes," said Lydia in her sweetest, most natural tone. "Turn on the light, Bobby, or you'll fall over something. It's just there on your right."

It took Bobby a moment to find the switch. When he turned on the light he saw Lydia and Albee sitting side by side on the sofa. Lydia was holding a folded paper in her hand.

"What's the point of sitting in here when the act is on?" said Bobby. "Let's go in and see her vamp the strong man."

Lydia sprang up, and looking at Albee deliberately tucked away the paper in the front of her low dress.

"Turn out the light again Bobby," she said. "It shines between the curtains and disturbs me."

All three went back to the box, where Miss Bennett had been sitting alone. It was a long time since Lydia had heard any music, and the music of the second act of Samson and Delilah, the long sweeping chords on the harp, began to trouble her, as the coming thunderstorm seemed to be troubling Delilah.

Her long abstraction from any artistic impression made her as susceptible as a child. The moonlight flooded her with a primitive glamour, her nerves crept to the music of the incredibly sweet duet; and when at last Samson followed Delilah into her house Lydia felt as if the soprano's triumph were her own.

As the storm broke Albee rose. He bent over Miss Bennett and then over Lydia.

"Good night, Delilah," he whispered.

148

She did not answer, but she thought, "Not to your Samson, Stephen Albee."

He was gone and she still had the letter. When the act was over she went back to the anteroom to read it. Yes, there it was on Simpson, Aspinwall & McCarter's heavy, simple stationery—clear and unequivocal. Mr. Simpson regretted so much that conditions had arisen which made it imperative—

Lydia glanced across the house and caught O'Bannon laughing at something that Eleanor was saying to him. She smiled. Whatever the joke was, she thought she knew a better one.

"How lovely you look, Lydia," said Bobby, seeing the smile. "Almost like a madonna in that white stuff—like a madonna painted by an Apache Indian."

"Have you anything that I could write on Bobby—a scrap of paper?"

Bobby tore out a page from a cherished address book and gave it to her with a gold pencil from his watch chain. She stood under the light, pressing the top of the pencil against her lips. Then she wrote rapidly:

"I have something of importance to say to you. Will you meet me in the lobby on the Thirty-ninth Street side at the end of the performance and let me drive you home?

"Lydia Thorne."

She folded it and held it out.

"Will you take that to O'Bannon and get an answer from him?"

"To O'Bannon?" said Bobby. "Has anything happened?"

"Don't bother me now, Bobby, there's a dear. Just take it." She half shoved him out of the box. "And be as quick as you can," she called after him.

He really was quick. In a few seconds she saw the curtain of the opposite box pushed aside and Bobby enter. He spoke a moment to Eleanor, and then when no one else was watching she saw him speak to O'Bannon and give him her note. The two men rose and went together into the back of the box out of her sight. What was happening? Was O'Bannon now on his way to her? There was a long delay. Miss Bennett's voice called, "Is somebody knocking?" The noise was Lydia's restless feet tapping on the floor. Just as the lights began to go down Bobby returned—alone. He handed her a note.

149

*"Dear Miss Thorne: I cannot drive home with you,
but I will stop at your house for a few minutes about half-
past eleven or a quarter to twelve, if that is not too late.
"D. O'B."*

Lydia smiled again. This was better still. She would have plenty of time in her own drawing-room to reveal the facts in any way she liked. She hardly heard the music of the next theme, hardly enjoyed the spectacle of Samson's degradation, so absorbed was she in the anticipation of the coming interview.

During the ballet in the last scene she saw Eleanor rise and O'Bannon follow her. She sprang up at once, though Miss Bennett faintly protested.

"Oh, aren't you going to wait to see him pull down the temple? It's such fun." Miss Bennett liked to see masculine strength conquer. Lydia shook her head, but offered no explanation.

It was almost half past eleven when they entered the house. Miss Bennett, who had been yawning on the drive home, walked straight to the staircase. Morson had delegated his duties for the evening to the parlor maid, a young Swede, and she began industriously drawing the bolts of the front door and preparing to put out the lights. Lydia stopped her.

"Get me a glass of water, will you, Frieda?" she said.

"There'll be one in your room, dear," Miss Bennett called back, every inch the housekeeper. She did not stop, however, but went on up and disappeared round the turn in the stairs.

When the girl came back Lydia said, "Frieda, I'm expecting a gentleman in a few minutes. After you've let him in you need not wait up. Is the fire lit in the drawing-room? Then light it, please."

She stood for a moment, sipping at the long, cool glass and listening to hear Miss Bennett's footsteps growing more and more distant; listening, too, for a footstep in the street.

In the drawing-room the firelight was already leaping up, outdoing the light of the shaded lamps. Left alone, Lydia slipped off her opera cloak very softly, as if she did not want to make the smallest noise that would interfere with her listening. The house was quiet, and even the noise of the city was beginning to die down. The steady roar of traffic returning from the theater was almost over. Now and then she could hear a Fifth Avenue bus rolling along on its heavy rubber tires; now and then the slamming of a motor door as some of her neighbors returned from an evening's amusement.

She bent over the fire trying to warm her hands. They were like ice, and it must have been from cold, not excitement, she

150

thought, for her mind felt as calm as a well. She turned the little clock—all lilac enamel and rhinestones—so that she could watch it's tiny face. It was a quarter to twelve. She clenched her hands. Did he intend to keep her waiting?

She started, for the door had softly opened. Miss Bennett entered in one of her gorgeous dressing gowns of crimson satin and bright-blue birds.

"Dear child," she said, "you ought to be in bed."

"I'm waiting for someone who's coming to see me, Benny; and as he may be here at any minute, and I don't suppose you want to be caught in your present costume—"

Miss Bennett lifted her shoulders.

"Oh, at my age!" she said. "After all, what is the use of having lovely dressing gowns if no one ever sees them?"

"It's Dan O'Bannon that's coming," said Lydia, "and I want to see him alone."

"O'Bannon coming here! But, Lydia, you can't see him alone—at this hour. Why, it's midnight!"

Miss Bennett's eyes clung to her.

"Eleven minutes to," said Lydia, with her eyes on the clock. "I wish you'd go, Benny."

Miss Bennett hesitated.

"I don't think you ought to see him alone. I don't think it's quite—quite nice."

"Oh, this is going to be very nice!"

"No, I mean I don't think it's safe. Suppose anything should happen."

"Should happen?" said Lydia, and for a moment she looked like the old haughty Lydia. "What could happen?"

Miss Bennett raised both her arms and let them drop with a gesture quite French, expressing that they both knew what men were.

"He might try to make love to you," she said.

The minute she had spoken she wished she had not, for Lydia's fine dark brow contracted.

"What disgusting ideas you do have Benny! That man!" She stopped herself. "I almost wish he would. If he did I think I should kill him."

To Miss Bennett this seemed just an expression; but to Lydia, with her eyes fixed on an enormous pair of steel-and-silver scissors that lay on the writing table, it was something more than a phrase.

Miss Bennett decided to withdraw.

"Stop in my room when you come up," she said. "I shan't close

151

my eyes till you do." Then gathering her shining draperies about her she left the room.

Even after Miss Bennett had gone her suggestion remained with Lydia. Would that man have any such idea? Would he think her sending for him at such an hour had any flattering significance? Or would he see that it was proof of her utter contempt for him—of her belief that she was his superior, the master mind of the two, whatever their situation? As for love-making—let him try it! Her blow would be all the more effective if it could be delivered while he was on his knees.

With an absurd, hurried, tingling stroke the little clock struck midnight. Strange, she thought, that waiting for something certain stretched the nerves more than uncertainty. She knew O'Bannon would come—or did she? Would he dare do that? Leave her sitting waiting for him and never come at all? Undoubtedly he had taken Eleanor back to her hotel. Were they laughing together over her note?

At that instant she heard the distant buzz of the front doorbell. Every nerve in her body vibrated at the sound. Then the drawing-room door opened and closed behind O'Bannon.

The fly had walked into the parlor, she said to herself—a great big immaculately attired fly. Seeing him there before her all her nervousness passed away, and she was conscious of nothing but joy—a joy as inspiring as if it were founded on something holier than hatred; joy that at last her moment had come.

She waited a second for his apology, and then she said quite in the manner of a great lady who without complaining is conscious of what is due to her, "You're late."

"I walked up," he said. "It's a lovely night."

"You have wondered why I sent for you?"

"Of course."

She sank lazily into a chair by the fire.

"Sit down," she said graciously, as if she were according the privilege to an old servant who might hesitate otherwise.

He shook his head.

"No," he answered; "I can't stay but a minute. It's after twelve."

He leaned his elbow on the mantelpiece and took up the jade dog that stood there, examining its polished surfaces. Lydia was well content with this arrangement. It made her feel more at ease. She let a silence fall, and in the silence he raised his eyes from the dog and looked at her as if he were reluctant to do so.

He said, "I'm glad to see you here—back in your normal surroundings."

152

Thank heaven she did not have to be dovelike any more.

"Oh, are you?" she said derisively. "Didn't you enjoy your little visit to me in prison?"

He shook his head slowly.

"Then may I ask why you came?"

"I don't think I shall tell you that."

"Do you think I don't know?" she asked with a sudden fierceness.

"I really haven't thought whether you knew or not."

"You came to get just what you did get—the full savor of the humiliation of my position."

"My God," he answered coolly, "and they say women have intuition!"

His tone, as much as his words, irritated her, and she did not want to be irritated. She raised her chin.

"It doesn't really matter why you came, at least not to me. Let me tell you why I sent for you to-night."

But he was pursuing his own train of thought and did not seem to hear her.

"Are you able to come back into life again? Are you"—he hesitated—"are you happy?"

"No. But then I never was very happy. I can tell you this: I wouldn't exchange my prison experience for anything in my whole life. You gave me something, Mr. O'Bannon, when you sent me to prison, that no one else was ever able to give me, not even my father, though he tried. I mean a sense of the consequences of my own character. That's the only aspect of punishment that is of use to people."

His eyes lit up.

"You don't mean you're grateful to me!" he said.

"No, not grateful," she answered, and a little smile began to curve the corners of her mouth. "Not grateful to you, because, you see, I am going to return the obligation—to do the same kind deed to you."

"To me? I don't believe I understand."

"I don't believe you do. But be patient. You will. During my trial, I imagine—in fact I was told by your friends—that you took the position that you were treating me as you treated any criminal whose case you prosecuted."

"What other stand could I take?"

"Oh, officially none. But in your mind you must have known you had another motive. Some people think it was a young man's natural thirst for headlines, but I know—and I want you to know I know it—that it was your personal vindictiveness toward me."

153

"Don't say that!" he interrupted sharply.

"I shall say it," Lydia went on, "and to you, because you are the only person I can say it to. Oh, you knew very well how it would be! I have to sit silent while Eleanor tells me how noble your motives were in prosecuting me. You know—oh, you are so safe in knowing—that I will not tell anyone that your hatred of me goes back to that evening when I did not show myself susceptible to your fascinations when you tried to kiss me, and I—"

"I did kiss you," said O'Bannon.

"I believe you did, but—"

"You know I did."

She sprang up at this.

"And is that something you're proud of, something it gives you satisfaction to remember?"

"The keenest."

She stamped her foot.

"That you kissed a woman against her will? Held her in your arms because you were physically stronger? You like to remember—"

"It was not against your will," he said.

"It was!"

"It was not!" he repeated. "Do you think I haven't been over that moment often enough to be sure of what happened? You were not angry! You were glad I took you in my arms! You would have been glad if I had done it earlier!"

"Liar!" said Lydia. "Liar and cad—to say such a thing!" She was shivering so violently that her teeth chattered like a person in an ague. "If you knew—if you could guess the repugnance, the horror of a woman embraced by a man she loathes and despises! Her flesh creeps! There are no words for it! And then—then to be told by that man's mad vanity that she liked it, that she wanted it, that she brought it on herself—"

"Just wait a moment," he said. "I believe that you hate me now all right, whatever you felt then."

"I do, I do hate you," she answered, "and I have the power of proving it. I can do you an injury."

"You will always have the power of injuring me."

"Be sure I will use it."

"I dare say you will."

"I have. I haven't wasted any time at all."

"What is all this about? What have you done?" he asked without much interest.

She drew the letter out of the front of her dress and handed it to him with a hand that trembled so much it made the folded paper
154

rattle. He took it, unfolded it, read it. Watching him, she saw no change in his face until he looked up and smiled.

"Is this it?" he asked. "A lot I care about that—not to go into the Simpson firm! You don't understand your power. The things that would have made me suffer—well, if you had let prison break you, if you had given your love to that crooked politician who came down to bribe me on your behalf—Why, when you fell at my feet in the reception room at Auburn I suffered more than in all my life before or since, because I love you."

"Stop!" said Lydia. "Don't dare say that to me!"

"I love you," he said. "You don't have to go about looking for things like this," and he flicked the letter contemptuously into the fire. "You make me suffer just by existing."

"I won't listen to you!" said Lydia, and she moved away.

"Of course you'll listen to me," he answered, standing between her and the door. "There isn't one thing you've done since I first saw you that has given me the slightest pleasure or peace or happiness—nothing but unrest and pain. When you're hard and bitter I suffer, and when you're gentle and kind—"

She gave a sort of laugh at this.

"When have you ever seen me gentle and kind?" she asked.

"Oh, I know how wonderfully you could give yourself to a man if you loved him."

"Don't say such things!" she said, actually shuddering. "It sickens me! Don't even think them!"

"Think! Good God, the things I think!"

"Don't even think of me at all except as your relentless enemy. If it were true what you just said now, that you love me—"

"It is true."

"I hope it is. It gives me more power to hurt you. It must make it worse for you to know how I hate, how I despise you, everything about you; your using your looks and your fine figure to hypnotize simple people like Eleanor and Miss Bennett and poor Evans; the vanity that makes you hate me for being free of your charms; and all the petty, underhanded things you did in the trial; all your sentimental buncombe with the poor little Wooley girl; and your twisting the law—the law that you are supposed to uphold—in order to get that bracelet before the jury; your mouthing and your cheap arts with the jury; and most of all your coming to Auburn to feast your eyes on my humiliation. Oh, if I could forgive all the rest I could never forgive you that!"

"I'm not particularly eager that you should forgive me," he said.

To her horror she found that the breaking down of the

155

barriers which had kept her all these months from rehearsing her grievances to anyone was breaking down her self-control. She knew she was going to cry.

"You can go now," she said. She made a sweeping gesture toward the door. Already the muscles in her throat were beginning to contract. He stood looking into the fire as if he had not heard her. She stamped her foot. "Don't you understand me?" she said. "I want you to go."

"I'm going, but there's something I want to say to you." He was evidently trying to think something out in words.

"I shall never have anything more to say to you," she replied.

She sank down on the sofa and leaned her head back among the cushions. She closed her eyes to keep back her tears, and sat rigid with the struggle. If she did not speak again—and she wouldn't—she might get rid of him before the storm broke. He took a cigarette and lit it. Even New York was silent for a minute, and the little clock on the table succeeded in making audible its faint, quick ticking. Lydia became aware that tears were slowly forcing their way under her lids, that she was swallowing audibly. She put her hands against her mouth in the effort to keep back a sob. And O'Bannon began to speak, without looking at her.

"I don't know whether I can make you understand," he said. "I don't know that it matters whether you understand or not, but in your whole case I did exactly what a district attorney ought to do, only it is true that behind my doing it—"

He was stopped by a sob.

"Yes, yes!" she said fiercely, her whole face distorted with emotion, "it's true I'm crying, but if you come near me I'll kill you."

"I won't," he answered. "Cry in peace."

She took him at his word. She cried, not peacefully but wildly. She flung herself face downward on the sofa and sobbed, with her head buried in the cushions, while her whole body shook. She had not cried like this since she was a little child. It was a wild luxurious abandonment of all self-control. Once she heard O'Bannon move.

"Don't touch me!" she repeated without raising her head.

"I'm not going to," he answered.

He began to walk up and down the room—up and down the room she could hear him going. Once he went to the mantelpiece, and leaning his elbows on the shelf he put his hands over his ears. And then without warning he came and sat down beside her on the sofa and gathered her into his arms like a child.

"No, no!" she said with what little was left of her voice.

"Oh, what difference does it make?" he answered.

She made no reply. She seemed hardly aware that he had

156

drawn her head and shoulders across his upright body so that her face was hidden in the crook of his arm. He put his hand on her heaving shoulder, looking down at the disordered knot of her black hair. A few minutes before he would have said that he could not have touched her hand without setting fire to his strong desire for her. And here she was, softly in his arms, and his only emotion was a tenderness so comprehensive that all desires beyond that moment were swallowed up in it.

He almost smiled to remember the futility of the explanation he had been attempting. This was the real explanation between them. How little difference words made, he thought, and yet how we all cling to them! He took his free hand from her shoulder, and like a careful nurse he slid back a hair-pin, just poised to fall from the crisp mass of her hair.

Gradually her sobs stopped, she gave a long deep breath, and presently he saw she had fallen asleep.

There never was an hour in O'Bannon's life that he set beside that hour. He sat like a man in a trance, and yet acutely aware of everything about him; of the logs in the fire that, burning through, fell apart like a blazing drawbridge across the andirons; of an occasional footstep in the street; and finally of the inevitable approach of the rattling milk wagon, of its stopping at the door, of the wire trays, of the raising of the Thorne basement window and the slow thump of the delivery of the allotted number of bottles.

After a long time a little frightened face stared at him round the door. Turning his head slowly, he saw Miss Bennett, her gray hair brushed straight back from her face and her eyes large and staring.

"Is she dead?" she whispered.

O'Bannon shook his head, and hardly making a sound, his lips formed the words, "Go away."

Miss Bennett really couldn't do that.

"It's almost five o'clock," she said reproachfully.

He nodded.

"Go away," he said.

In her bright satin dressing gown she sat down, but he could see that she was nervous and uncertain. He summoned all the powers of will that he possessed; he fixed his eyes on her, compelling her to look at him; and when he felt he had gathered her in he raised his right hand and gently but decisively pointed to the door. She got up and went out.

The fire had burned itself completely out now, and the cold of the hours before dawn began to penetrate the room. O'Bannon began to apprehend the fact that this night must some time end—

that Lydia must presently wake up. He dreaded the moment there would be more anger, more repudiation of the obvious bond between them, more torture and separation. He shivered, and leaning forward he softly drew her cloak from a neighboring chair and laid it over her, tucking it in about her shoulders. He was afraid the movement might have waked her, but she seemed to sleep on.

Again the minutes began to slip enchantedly away, and then far away in the house, in some remote upper story, he heard a footstep. Housemaids. Inwardly be called down the curse of heaven upon them. He glanced down at Lydia, and suddenly knew—how he knew it he could not say—that she had heard it too; that she had been awake a long time, since he put the cloak over her—perhaps since Miss Bennett had left the room.

Awake and content! His heart began to beat loudly, violently.

"Lydia," he said.

She did not move or answer, only he felt that her head pressed more closely into the hollow of his arm.

THE END

158

www.ingramcontent.com/pod-product-compliance
Lightning Source LLC
Chambersburg PA
CBHW011510170626
46810CB00009B/3312